An Alpha's Promise

BOOK ONE IN THE HUND VALLEY SERIES

KITT LYNN

LUPO PUBLISHING

The Enchanted Lands of Havre

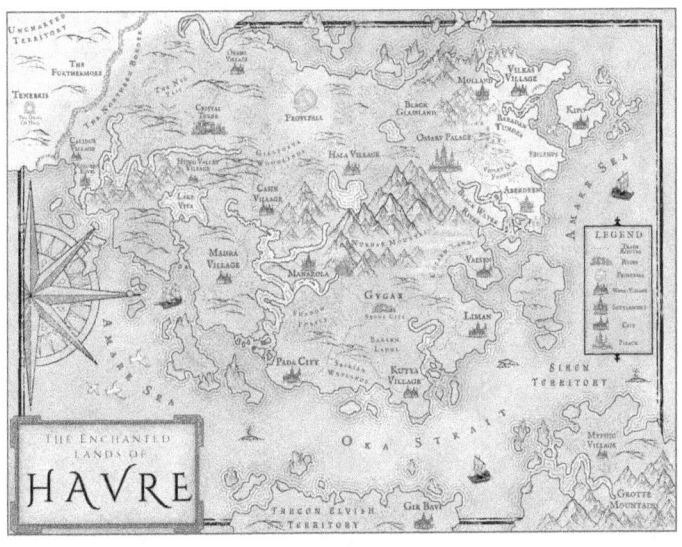

To see a larger version of the map of Havre, visit www. kittlynn.com.

For my Bryce.

The Omega Origins

IT HAS BEEN SAID that hundreds of years ago, werewolves roamed free, dominating the land and all other creatures. Men that easily slipped into their wolf form at will, they were savage and unforgiving. Destroying anything that crossed their paths.

Humans kept their distance from the unhinged animals until a young noblewoman found herself lost in the enchanted forests. A werewolf found her and they fell in love, and she birthed twins. The first Beta and Omega.

The Omega, unable to transform into its wolf, was a gentle creature, fragile and obedient. The perfect mate for the more aggressive Alpha werewolf.

The Beta had more beastly characteristics but could only shift into its wolf when the Moon hung at her fullest. Calm and smart, the child held the perfect balance between human and wolf.

The birth was hard and bloody, and the noblewoman died, her body unable to handle the horrors of birthing beasts. But she left behind a new breed of weres, creating a fragile balance between wolf and man.

The villages grew, bursting with werewolves of all kinds:

Alphas, Betas, and Omegas. And soon, the humans realized the wolves finally had a weakness. Their mates, the Omegas.

The humans attacked, slaughtering hundreds of the gentle creatures, pushing werewolves almost to the point of extinction until the fairylands came to their rescue. Fighting the humans and staving them off. Reclaiming Havre as a land of enhancement and magic.

To protect their kind from any further attacks, the Alphas locked their Omegas away in villages fortified with large border walls, shutting them in and keeping them safe.

The Casin Gardens

Emmy

"SANA!" I whispered as loudly as I could without making too much noise. Taking another quick look at the dashing Alpha in the distance, I frantically waved her over.

My sister turned away from a cluster of pink rose bushes and glanced to where I pointed. Hunkering down, she hurried toward me, trying to keep her golden locks hidden beneath the perfectly manicured bushes.

"I think he's here!" I said with a restrained squeal.

A tall, young Alpha dismounted a steed at the front of the packhouse. His bulky muscles flexed under his fitted, deep blue shirt, and his dark hair was a little long, touching his ears and hanging into the corners of his eyes. He looked like every love story I had ever read.

Sana settled next to me and peeked her head up.

I hoped he couldn't see us from where we hid in the

3

garden. While we were a good distance away, we were still easy for an Alpha to spot. Their eyesight was like no other beast in Havre.

Sana moved carefully, barely catching a glance before falling back down. After all, it was forbidden for them to see each other before the ceremony.

"Is that him?" I whispered.

"Maybe. I don't know what he looks like," she said. The corners of her full lips turned slightly down.

Their mating had been arranged since birth. And, for some reason, she had spent her whole life willing herself to learn as little as possible about her Alpha and his village. It baffled me.

Her prince was here to claim her. How could she not be bursting with joy?

"Should we move closer? Get a better look?" I cooed, nudging my nose into her cheek.

"Emmy," she groaned, leaning away. "Mother would kill me if she knew I was this close."

I craned my neck up, stealing another look.

My parents and older brother greeted the handsome wolf and, who I assumed was his father, the Hund Valley Pack Alpha. Both were very tall, with similar features—same shaggy, dark hair curled slightly at the ends, sharp jawlines, and broad shoulders. The only noticeable difference was Sana's soon-to-be mate's rounded cheeks and full head of hair compared to his father's thinning crown.

"Emmy," Sana whispered, pulling at the hem of my dress and motioning for me to duck back down.

I relented and slumped next to her in the soft grass. "What's wrong?" I asked, squeezing her arm. "Why aren't you excited?"

She had become so distant and secluded as the ceremony neared, and I just didn't understand.

This was her chance to leave Casin and start a new life. I wanted nothing more than to mate a dashing stranger from a far-off land, be whisked away, then worshiped and adored for the rest of my life. If it were me, I'd be dancing with joy.

"Please, Sana," I whined. "Tell me what's wrong."

She sighed long and hard, pulling a rosebud off the bush next to us and plucking its petals. She rubbed them between her fingers before letting them fall, crushed and torn, to the ground.

"I just don't want to do this," she mumbled.

"Why not?" I asked, much louder than intended.

"Sana? Omega Emmy?"

I jerked at the deep voice and tried to curl into myself.

Sana glared at me, pulling her lips into a tight line and scrunching up her nose in anger.

I mouthed a quick '*sorry*'.

She rolled her eyes, defeated, and stood up. "Lieutenant Andrus," she sighed.

"Sana!" the Alpha yelled in a firm, disapproving tone. His voice boomed through the otherwise serene garden. "Where is—"

I slowly stood up next to my sister, and he narrowed his eyes at me, his pointed features tight with frustration. It made my wolf whimper.

He let out a quick huff then gestured for us to follow. His usually stiff, slick black hair looked less than perfect, and his cheeks were flushed. It made me smile to think of him panicking when he found us missing.

Sana and I just wanted to enjoy what little time we had left together in the sun, not locked in a stuffy parlor all day.

Andrus opened the side door to the packhouse and marched inside, not holding it open or waiting for us to enter. He lumbered down the hallway, moving briskly, the scent of anger pouring off his shoulders.

The voices of our visitors drifted toward me, and I paused, glancing down a corridor toward my father's study. The two Hund Valley Alphas stood talking to my mother. Sana's new mate channeled his fingers through his dark hair, and his lips pulled into a friendly smile.

Sana was so lucky, even if she refused to see it.

Andrus cleared his throat, standing just in front of the parlor door at the end of the hallway. I raced toward him, hoping he'd move. But true to form, he stood firm in the doorway. I angled myself sideways to edge around the Alpha, the heat of his body making my skin crawl, and I swore I heard him scent me as I moved under his eyes. Darting to the other side of the room, I pushed myself onto the couch, hiding from his cold glare.

Sana sauntered in slowly, bumping hard into Andrus' arm. The Alpha pressed his lips into a thin line and exhaled hard.

He was young for his rank, maybe his mid-twenties or so, but his overly stern appearance made him look much older and incredibly mean. Everything the Alpha did had an air of hostility to it, as if he was always on the verge of losing control.

Simply being in his presence made my wolf a nervous wreck.

Andrus' narrowed his eyes at Sana, and his fists shook as he gently pressed the door closed. His actions were calm and controlled, but his hard hands and tense jaw betrayed his anger.

Sana watched him carefully, raising an eyebrow when he pushed his back against the door and stood at attention.

"I get it," she said to the guard, draping her long, slender body over an oversized armchair. "We fucked up, but there's no need to stand inside the room. We'll stay put."

"You'll forgive me if I don't believe you," he snapped.

She met his glare, not blinking. The air in the room grew thick and hot until he finally relented and looked away. His fierce eyes drifted over my face for a quick moment before he turned his attention back to the wall across from him.

I hated that my father placed so much trust in him to guard us.

"Andrus!" Sana snapped, her posture tight and commanding. "My sister and I don't have much time together. I want time *alone* with her before I depart for Hund Valley tomorrow. Leave."

"Your father ordered me to watch you," his shoulders tensed, and his teeth flashed as he spoke. "I trusted you to stay put, and you both disappeared. Alpha Hector would have my head if he found out, and I will *not* be fool enough to let you out of my sight again."

"I don't give a shit what my father ordered." She jumped to her feet, and my wolf whimpered long and hard. "I want to be alone with my sister. Get out!"

I used to pray to the Moon I'd one day be as impressive and commanding as Sana. Even though we were only a handful of years apart, I couldn't help but always feel so small and weak in her presence.

I wanted to be like her. A fierce she-Alpha to be respected and envied. But as an Omega, my dreams of being statuesque and feared were far-fetched at best. I was small, fidgety, and easily spooked. At least, that's how my father always described me.

"You should be kept as far away from Omega Emmy as possible," Andrus gritted out, stepping forward. "It's a blessing that you'll be gone soon."

"What the fuck does that mean?" She bared her teeth.

I pushed my face into a pillow in an effort to shield myself from their thick emotions.

Their anger pulsed around me, making my wolf whine and my eyes burn. Wrapping a strand of my hair around my finger, I twisted it repeatedly, trying to block out their rage.

"Your wicked attitude and loose tongue are a horrible example for the Omega." He glanced at me before returning his steely, grey eyes to Sana. "You may be comfortable mouthing off to every Alpha that comes your way, but to do it in front of her is reckless. One wrong word to the wrong wolf and Omega Emmy could be killed in the blink of an eye. You should be teaching her how to hold her tongue, not wield it like a blade!"

"I'm a horrible example?" Sana laughed, placing her hand dramatically over her chest. "Emmy? Did you hear that? I'm a horrible example! All the shit wolves in this packhouse, and I'm the fucking problem!" She continued to mock Andrus, making the Alpha's nostrils flare.

I pushed myself into the mountain of pillows, wishing they'd leave me alone. I just wanted to go to my room and cry in private.

"Andrus," she let out a long, loud sigh, "what I do or don't do, say or don't say in front of Emmy is none of your business. Now fuck off," she clicked her tongue, giving the Alpha a wicked grin.

Andrus took a careful step toward Sana, challenging her with his every movement, but she held firm. She didn't move, flinch, or blink. She was amazing.

"You think you can't be put in your place because you're a member of the Pack Alpha's family?" he seethed, his tone deep and scary. "Be careful, Sana. One day you'll piss off the wrong wolf, and there will be no one to save your pampered ass."

"How dare you speak to me like this!" She bared her teeth, pushing a harsh growl from her throat.

"S-stop!" I sobbed, their rage completely overwhelming all

my senses. It filled my nose and burned my lungs, and I couldn't take anymore. "Please!"

"Emmy," Sana whispered, suddenly at my side. She wrapped her arms around me and snuggled me close, all her anger gone. "I'm so sorry, sweetheart. I wasn't thinking."

I pushed myself into my sister's soft hair and peaked up at her. She looked upset, trying to soothe my distress. Andrus struggled to regain his composure. I watched his shoulders rise and fall with each labored breath before he finally moved back to the door, each step seeming to take great effort.

I let out a heavy breath as the air in the room eased and both their tempers deflated.

"Sana! Emmy!"

Our mother's shrill voice sliced through the door and filled the room. Andrus jumped and immediately grabbed the doorknob, pulling it open in a quick, almost frantic manner.

My mother stepped into the room wearing one of her best dresses. Her sandy-blonde hair was tucked in its signature stiff bun, and her cheeks were a calculating shade of pink that perfectly complimented her beaded necklace and bracelet.

"It's getting late, and you both will need your rest for tomorrow," she said, her voice flat and posture stiff—like always. "Go to your rooms."

I leaned forward and glanced out the window to see the sun only just touching the tops of the trees. It was too early to go to bed, but my mother was not the kind of Alpha that tolerated backtalk. She was stern and unforgiving even when slightly challenged. I was amazed the woman could cultivate enough body warmth to create three children, let alone gather the passion to make them.

"Sana, walk with me," she said sweetly, but we both knew better. It wasn't a request, nor was it sweet. "Andrus." She turned to the Lieutenant. He snapped to attention, ready for his orders. "Take Emmy to her room."

"Yes, Luna Morana."

Their eyes met and lingered for a moment, something odd exchanging between them. My mother nodded and squeezed his shoulder before turning to my sister.

He gave both of them a low bow before cutting his eyes to me, narrowing them ever so slightly.

The Casin Packhouse

Emmy

I COULD FEEL ANDRUS' eyes on me the whole way to my room. He was so close it felt as if he was breathing on my neck, making the skin along my spine prickle.

Walking slowly through the hallway, each step deliberate and forced, I tried to keep my nerves from overtaking me. My wolf begged me to run as fast as possible from the Alpha.

There was just something about him that set my whole body on edge.

"Omega," Andrus said as we entered the long hallway toward my bedroom. He quickened his pace to walk beside me. "I'm glad I have you alone. I wanted to speak with you before the ceremony tomorrow, but I'm not sure if we'll have time in the morning."

I stiffened, not responding or turning to look at him. Instead, I concentrated on my feet and closing the distance to my bedroom door, which suddenly felt very far away.

"I apologize you were forced to witness such disrespect from your sister."

He spoke with so much arrogance it almost knocked me over, but I didn't respond, keeping my eyes on the end of the hallway.

"I want you to know," he continued, "that I don't hold her behavior against you. I know you would never act that way towards someone of authority."

I tensed with each word that fell from his mouth, wanting to remind him that he held no authority over me or my sister. And that Sana wasn't the disrespectful one.

As an Omega, I had no right to believe myself superior to anyone, especially an Alpha, but there were rules of conduct when it came to the Pack Alpha's family, and Andrus had crossed more than one line today.

I wanted to tell the Alpha his behavior was inexcusable, but I couldn't even bring myself to look him in the eye, let alone challenge whatever authority he thought he held.

How I wished I had Sana's courage. She would have corrected his attitude twice already.

Andrus grabbed my arm and pulled me to a stop right in front of my room. "Omega Emmy," he whispered. I was sure he meant it to come off as intimate, but it was just frightening; his piercing eyes, stiff manner, and imposing body made my wolf want to run. "Please know that when you are mine," he whispered, "I will treat you with the utmost respect."

Dread slipped down my spine. *When I am his?*

I shook my head slightly and backed up, my feet bumping into my bedroom door. "What?" I asked, unable to keep my voice from shaking. His dominance was too overwhelming, making my wolf shiver.

"I have asked your parents for permission to lay a claim on you, and both have agreed." His lips pulled slightly at the corners, his face twisting into a tight smile.

Once again, tears blurred my vision, and I hated myself for it. I should be screaming that I wasn't his and never would be, but instead, I just stood there, my silent rage dripping down my cheeks.

How could my parents do this to me without even asking?

I tucked my hands behind my back and fumbled to find the doorknob. "Alpha," I whispered, too frightened to speak any louder. The Alpha's anger lingered in the air around him, feeding into my panic. "I don't think...."

The look in his eyes locked me in place. It was intense and scary, like he wanted to eat me from the inside out. Suddenly frantic to get away, I turned the knob behind me and opened the door. But before I could shut it, he pushed his way inside the room with me.

He spun me hard, shoving my back against the door as it slammed shut. The knob dug into my spine, knocking all the air out of my lungs. Tears poured freely down my face as pain radiated up my body, throbbing at the base of my skull.

"Emmy," he growled, pushing his face into my neck and licking my skin.

I placed my trembling hands on his chest and tried to push him back, but he stayed firm against my body, not giving me an inch to move or breathe. Fear consumed me, and I tried again to shove him away, but he pressed himself harder, dragging his teeth over my skin. I froze, terrified he would try to mark me, to create a bond by force.

I choked on his harsh scent of pine mixed with something sickly sweet. It burned my eyes and throat, making each breath painful.

A whine slipped from high in my throat, and he leaned back, smiling.

"I have waited so long to have you," he said, wiping at my wet cheeks.

"Ah-alpha," I choked on a sob, trying to calm my body enough to speak. "Please—"

He gripped my face and crashed his lips to mine so hard I could taste a faint trace of blood. I gagged and tried to move my head away, but he met my movements, forcing my mouth open. His tongue pushed past my lips, despite how hard I tried to escape. I wanted to break away from him and scream the whole house down, but his hold on me was too tight.

So I gave up.

My hands fell limp at my sides as I stared at the trees just outside my window while he assaulted my mouth. The green leaves danced in the wind, rustling and swaying rhythmically.

I closed my eyes, wishing I was still in the garden, smelling the sweet flowers and feeling the wind on my face.

Andrus grunted, pulling me back to his kiss and the feel of his body against mine. The doorknob was still grinding into my back, sharp and painful.

After what felt like an eternity, he pulled away, finally getting his fill. His eyes were hooded and laced with something terrifying. Swallowing convulsively, I wanted to throw up from the feel of his spit still in my mouth.

He stole my first kiss.

I pushed down the urge to claw at his eyes, knowing full well he could kill me without even trying. I wanted him to feel as weak and disgusting as I did.

I hated him, and I'd rather die than be forced to mate him.

Andrus inhaled the air around me and hummed, seemingly unaware of my distress. Or maybe he just didn't care. Slowly, he brought his lips to my temple and kissed the side of my face. I remained frozen, waiting for him to finish.

"Emmy," he growled, pushing himself closer to me, the doorknob practically fusing with my spine.

Something hard poked at my belly, and I realized with a

start what it was. This was what my parents had spent years warning me about and claiming to want to protect me from. And now here he was, the threat to steal my innocence stood in my bedroom, on my mother's orders.

"Andrus," I said, trying to summon all my courage. He was on the brink of losing control, and once he did, there was nothing I would be able to do to stop him. "I'm not of age yet." It was the only thing I could think to say.

He groaned, letting out a quick puff of air through his pursed lips before pushing his hands up into my hair. His fingers tangled in my tresses and pulled. Despite how hard I tried to stay silent, I grunted from the slight pain.

"Andrus," I said again, wishing I was stronger. "Please, please let me go."

He stayed pushed against me, his lips on my forehead, my back pressed into the unforgiving door. He didn't move, just remained utterly still—his body flush against mine. I was too frightened to move or say anything else. So instead, I focused on not crying.

Letting out a rumbling sigh, his body trembled slightly. I assumed he was trying to regain control over himself, or at least that's what I prayed.

"Emmy," he rasped out, clearing his throat roughly. With slow movements, he removed his hands from my body and took a step back, smoothing down the front of his shirt.

I stayed pushed against the door, not trusting that I was allowed to move.

"Emmy," he said again, louder and more in control, finally meeting my eyes. "I apologize. You're right. You aren't of age yet. I shouldn't have lost myself. Of course, our bonding won't take place until after you turn twenty. I've waited all these years. I can wait a few more weeks." His lips pulled into that creepy, painful smile. I just stared back, not acknowledging his words.

He reached out for me, and I flinched, shutting my eyes and turning away from him. He chuckled as he grabbed my hand.

I squeezed my eyes tighter, waiting.

"My sweet Omega." His voice oozed as he kissed my palm. "I forget just how fragile you creatures are." His fingers brushed down the side of my face.

"I should go," he said. "But first, a gift."

I opened my eyes and held my breath, terrified of what he considered a *gift*. He reached for his belt and pulled out a small book bound in a bright yellow fabric, setting it carefully in my hand.

"I know how much you enjoy stories," he smiled as if winning a hard-fought game. "Sleep well, my Omega."

I jumped, moving away from the door and pressing tight into the nearest corner. I watched as he stepped into the hallway but not before turning to give me one more sickening smile. The second the door clicked behind him, I let out a heavy sob, dropping the book and wiping at my mouth with both hands.

I slowly slid to the floor. My whole body hurt, and the taste of blood and his saliva still sat in my mouth.

My dreams of finding a handsome, loving, and passionate mate turned to dust, and I choked on the realization that I was going to be bound to Andrus.

My heart broke, and I sobbed long and hard until my tears dried up and exhaustion finally took me.

Emmy's Bedroom

Emmy

"WHAT THE HELL ARE YOU DOING?"

My mother's voice ripped through my dreams.

I was still sitting in the corner of my bedroom floor, head tipped back against the wall. My back ached, and the skin on my cheeks was tight with dried tears, making my face itchy.

My mother fumed down at me. Her sandy-blonde hair wasn't in its usual bun but instead flowed down her back, frizzy and untamed. She adjusted her robe and pulled at the cincture around her waist, agitation rolling off her.

"Get up," she ordered.

Slowly I stood, my muscles stiff and knees shaky. She huffed when I didn't move quickly enough for her, and she grabbed my wrist, dragging me out of my bedroom and down the hall.

She flung open Sana's bedroom door and ushered me inside. My brother, father, and the commander of his guards stood in the center of the room, looking very serious and showing varying degrees of rage.

I looked around the room, finding Andrus standing at attention next to the door. His stiff demeanor softened as his eyes met mine, giving me a crooked, knowing smirk. I looked away, my stomach heaving from last night's memories.

My brother fumed, standing silently, but my father pulsated a rage I had never felt before. It made my wolf cower, and chest tighten.

"Did you know about this?" My father rushed toward me and grabbed my wrist. I stumbled backward as he met each of my steps, moving me faster into the wall and pinning me in place. "Did you know?" he roared.

"Father." Davon placed a hand on his shoulder and pulled him away from me. "Allow me."

My brother was never outright cruel to me, but he was never really kind either. He was a jerk, running on pure instinct and always ready for a fight, sometimes even creating one when boredom overtook him. While he frequently spoke down to me and taunted me, he never yelled or hit me. I was thankful for that.

"Emmy," Davon said, leaning down to look me in the eye. Something he always did when he was about to scold me. "Where is Sana? Tell us where she went, and you can return to your room."

I furrowed my brow and glanced around. Sana's bed was made, the quilt tucked snug at the corners, and her bathrobe was draped over the chair at her vanity. It looked as if she hadn't slept here last night.

"Emmy!" my mother snapped when I didn't answer fast enough.

"I don't know," I choked out. "Last time I saw her was in the parlor."

"I told you she'd be useless," my mother groaned, turning away from me. My father shook his head in disappointment.

"Maybe she's in the gardens," I whispered, trying to ease the intensity swirling around me.

"She's not in the fucking gardens!" my father spat.

I looked to Davon, not understanding why everyone was so angry.

"Sana ran away last night," he said as if reading my mind. I shook my head, confused. "Where is she, Emmy?" he asked again, his tone harder.

"No," I whispered, my mind swirling with chaos and fear. I shifted my gaze between my parents, both equally furious. "She wouldn't do that. Someone took her. She wouldn't just run away." I didn't realize I was yelling until my brother grabbed me by the shoulders and shook me hard.

"Calm down!" he demanded over my harsh sobs.

The Omega in me forced me silent against my better judgment. I pressed myself more firmly against the wall, desperate to escape the room filled with so many hostile wolves.

"She left, Emmy," my mother sighed pointedly, shoving a small torn piece of paper in my hand. It was simple. Just a few words.

sorry I can't. - Sana

I read it and re-read it, then read it again. It was her handwriting.

My parents started talking amongst themselves, the prelude to what I assumed would be a fierce argument, but I couldn't focus on their words. I was busy looking around the room, not even sure what I was looking for. Evidence of a struggle? Blood? A ransom note? I didn't know. But I needed something that told me she was really gone and that she left by her own two feet.

My parents' voices raised, and their gestures intensified behind me as I stepped in front of Sana's vanity. Various items to prepare herself for the bonding ceremony were strewn about, cluttering the small space. I shifted a few flowers and picked up her jade and pearl music box. It contained all her most prized possessions; various pieces of gifted jewelry, a small pocket of coins, and a ring from our grandmother. I held my breath and opened it.

It was empty.

My knees gave out, and I slumped onto the small, cushioned chair. I covered my mouth, hoping to contain the scream that wanted to burst out of me.

She left me.

Sana really left me.

"She's not ready, Hector," my mother said, her high-pitched voice demanding my attention.

"Fucking hell, Morana! I don't give two shits if she's ready or not. This is happening!" His chest rumbled as he paced. "We don't have a fucking choice."

His eyes caught mine, and he moved across the room, his long legs bringing him to me in only a few steps. Then he stopped, lowering his head to my level.

"Emmy," he snapped. He let out a forced breath, collecting his thoughts and trying to steady himself. He constantly did this when speaking to me, and it never actually calmed him. "I know how fond you are of Andrus," he said, his voice still far too loud.

My eyes went wide, and I struggled to stifle a snort. While it didn't surprise me he believed that—he rarely saw me and spoke to me even less—it was still laughable. But I just didn't understand why we were talking about Andrus.

"However," he continued, a look of determination on his

face, "there's just nothing else we can do. You'll have to take Sana's place."

Andrus's head snapped up at his words, a soft growl pushing from his chest. His reaction was so startling. I had never seen him challenge my father in anything, always the perfect and obedient guard. It was so shocking. I almost didn't register what my father had said.

I have to take Sana's place.

I swallowed hard, realization hitting me like a smack to the face. My feet bounced my knees up in a frantic manner, and my palms went slick with sweat. I had no idea how to be a mate. Sana had prepared her whole life to be the Hund Valley Luna. She had been instructed for years on how to be a perfect mate for the perfect Alpha. I wasn't even old enough to be claimed yet.

Looking up at my mother, I wanted to beg her not to make me do this, but my words stuck to the inside of my throat.

The idea of mating a handsome Alpha and living happily ever after was all I ever wanted in life, but this was too real. Too scary. And I was too young.

My mother knelt in front of me and took my hands in hers. It was such a caring gesture and so out of character. She nodded briefly before turning to my father.

"She'll be ready," she said in a firm tone. "Now leave. Emmy needs to prepare for her bonding ceremony."

Sana's Bedroom

Emmy

I SAT AT THE VANITY, hypnotized by the fluid movement
of the maids around me. They pulled all kinds of things out of
the wardrobe, puffing and smoothing an elegant, green gown
over the bed, and placing very fancy undergarments on the
settee. They were deep red and tiny. I had never seen anything
so ridiculous and doubted they would cover even half my
bottom.

"Emmy," my mother snapped her fingers in my face to pull
my attention to her. I went stiff, taking in her stern
expression.

She forced a smile, then spoke softly. "I know this isn't
ideal, and you're still very young, but you can do this. It's just a
ceremony." Her voice was laced with an edge of sadness or
something like that. It was so hard to tell. Outside of annoyance and anger, my mother wasn't very good at showing her
feelings.

"Tonight," she cleared her throat and stared at my hands clasped firmly in my lap. "Tonight, your mate might expect...*something*...from you." She looked as if each word was more painful than the last. "He might want to...touch you." She paused, looking up to meet my eyes. She waited as if expecting me to say something.

"Okay," I whispered, nodding.

Then it hit me.

Panic and fear flooded my chest, and my lips went numb. I wasn't old enough for this. How could they expect me to do this?

"Do you know what I'm saying?" she asked, a slight grimace on her face.

"Yes," I mumbled, widening my eyes to keep my tears from falling. If I cried, she'd be livid.

Pressing my lips together to try to force some feeling back into them, I pushed away the thought of what was expected of me. I hadn't thought of what would happen after the ceremony. I hadn't even had time to think about the actual ceremony itself.

My favorite books always depicted blushing Omegas with fluttering nerves and longing hearts. I was just terrified. How could I be expected to lay with someone I had never met?

The urge to cry flared up again, but I forced it down. Sana's apprehension suddenly made so much sense, and I felt so awful for judging her as I did.

"Good," my mother said sharply, tapping the back of my hand before stepping away to look over the maids' work.

Sana's ceremonial dress was laid out and her jewelry ready to place on her...on me.

"Just do what your Alpha says, okay?" She ran her hands over the delicate, deep green material. "It's your job as his mate to do what he wants."

I twisted my fingers together, trying to collect the courage to tell her that I wasn't ready to be someone's mate. I knew she wouldn't care, but I needed it known before it was too late.

"I don't want to do this," I mumbled, keeping my eyes on the carpet just next to my feet.

"Okay," she said, shocking the hell out of me. I snapped my head up, my mouth slightly ajar. "Let's go tell your father, and he can let the Hund Valley wolves know. Of course, it will probably start a war. We have an agreement, after all.

"Hundreds of our pack members will be forced to fight and will probably be slaughtered, and it will take generations to rebuild our village. But if you aren't in the mood, that's all that matters."

She glared at me, her cold eyes sharp and challenging. It was good to know the she-wolf in front of me would never change. And as bizarre as it was, I found a bit of comfort in that.

I lowered my eyes back to the floor and nodded.

She clicked her tongue before striding out of the room.

THE MIRROR REFLECTED a girl that looked vaguely familiar. Sana's green dress was tight and shiny, the material stretching across my middle. My cheeks glowed a vibrant shade of pink to hide my pale complexion, and my lips were a deep red.

One of the maids finished twisting my hair into tight, perfect ringlets that fell over my shoulders. Then she placed pretty, pink flowers to form a delicate crown perched on top of my head.

I looked like a less remarkable version of my sister.

We had the same rounded nose and heart-shaped face. But my brown eyes were nothing compared to her blue ones, and neither was my less than striking figure.

I pressed my hands to my hips, trying to squeeze the dress into a more natural shape. It hung a little awkwardly, not tailored to my measurements. Sana had a stunning shape. Curvy in all the right places with a tiny waist and long legs. I was very short, with a much less alluring build, but the dress seemed to help a bit in that regard.

I ran my hands over the embroidered flowers that decorated the bodice, loving how the golden details shimmered in the light. It was a beautiful dress, long and sleeveless, and the tight corset was kind enough to give me the illusion of a much fuller bust.

The girl in the mirror looked like a full-grown Omega. A soon-to-be mated Omega. I sucked in a nervous breath, realizing again that I was about to be bonded, and suddenly the dress didn't feel as silky or smooth.

"You look very pretty, Omega Emmy," one of the maids beamed.

I nodded in thanks and gave her the best smile I could muster.

"Emmy!" my mother gasped as she entered the room. She wore a flowing purple dress that hugged her form in a very tasteful manner, and her hair was in its usual bun. She beamed at me, pressing her hand to her chest in a dramatic fashion. "My pup! You look so beautiful!"

She grabbed my hands and held my arms out to get a better look. She eyed the blooming bruise on my wrist where Father had grabbed me but didn't say anything about it.

"Turn around," she ordered, dropping my hands and forcing me into a spin. "It's a little long, but there's no time to do anything about that," she mused, pressing her lips together. "But I think it's safe to say there's no way your new mate will be rejecting you."

I was stunned for a moment, not knowing rejection was an option. Maybe I would get lucky, and this Alpha would take one look at me, laugh, then head home. But then my mind drifted to Andrus and his snake-like tongue.

No. Life with a perfect stranger seemed preferable.

"Okay, Emmy." Her smile instantly faded, and her posture stiff. "It's time."

Blood rushed in my ears, and my heart thumped hard in my chest. I was sure everyone in the room could hear my roaring pulse as I slowly moved my feet toward the door. The maids whispered praises, and the bedroom door opened to display the hallway lined with servants and guards. Each one bowed low at my feet as I passed, and the guards moved to fall in line behind me.

It was so overwhelming to have so many eyes on me, and it only got worse when I stepped into the main entryway. Kitchen staff, gardeners, and service Betas cut a path to the front door, again bowing as I moved through the crowd. My eyes moved over everyone, settling on one of the cooks. She looked so proud but sad at the same time. She was always so kind to me.

My bare feet hit the dirt path outside, and I paused.

The whole village flanked the road before me, smiling and murmuring with adoration in their eyes. Despite the mass of weres, I felt so alone and exposed, my wolf whimpering within me. I tried to force a smile, wanting to be the kind of Omega they could be proud of, but, more than anything, I just wanted to cry.

The dirt kicked up beneath my feet as I made the long walk to the temple. My heart squeezed in my chest at the realization it was the last time I would walk on Casin Village's soil, an intensional tradition for wolves leaving our village for their mate's home.

I could hear the occasional pup crying or laughing, their parents shushing and scolding them. I didn't react, holding my head high and keeping the temple's roof in sight.

My mother's gaze burned into my back, pushing me toward my new future, my new mate.

Two guards stood on either side of the temple's heavy, double doors. The intense red color suddenly felt menacing and evil. The once familiar space held an air of uncertainty and fear that made my throat tighten, and I trembled slightly as the doors were pulled open.

The Hund Vally wolf stood at the end of the aisle, plush with a beautiful emerald green carpet. His deep blue robes fitted his firm build perfectly, displaying his strength and size, and his dark eyes narrowed as I moved slowly toward him.

Then suddenly, I realized I didn't even know his name.

The Bonding Ceremony

Rin

I TIGHTENED MY FISTS, clenching and unclenching, as I waited to lay my eyes on my new mate. I had spied her briefly yesterday being led through the gardens by a stern-looking guard. She was lovely even at a distance, tall, blonde, and almost regal looking, exactly as her mother had described. I was in no doubt that she would provide beautiful, strong pups.

The crowd outside swelled, and I straightened my back. My blue dress robes suddenly seemed too hot and heavy in the tight space.

My eyes found my father in the front row. He sat, surrounded by prestigious Casin pack members, who filled the small temple leaving only standing room for several. He nodded at me before pulling out a flask and taking a quick sip.

For a brief moment, I wished my mother were still alive and standing with me. She always brought me so much comfort, and the last year without her had been more than difficult. Shaking my head, I pushed the thoughts away and looked intently at the red doors, waiting for them to open.

I didn't want to admit how nervous I was, but this was my fate, claiming the beautiful creature just outside those blazing, red doors. Though I didn't feel ready, there was no helping it. It was my duty to seal this alliance and bring a promise of peace between both our packs. Our union would strengthen our bonds across the lands, making both stronger.

The bells just outside the temple rang loudly throughout the otherwise silent room. A stiff valet standing next to the door snapped to attention, and his voice rang out, loud and clear. "Presenting Omega Emyanna, daughter of the Casin Village Pack Alpha, Hector."

I furrowed my brow briefly. I thought my new mate was an Alpha, not an Omega, and her name definitely wasn't Emyanna. But before I could dwell on it too much, the doors pulled open.

A short, brown-haired pup stood in the entryway. She glanced at my face, her large, brown eyes filled with so much fear, before casting them down quickly. Her green and gold dress appeared too tight, making her movements stiff and forced, and her hands trembled as she pulled the fabric up to walk better.

This pup was not the mate promised. I was sure of it. My eyes found my father, and he leaned back against the pew, giving me an approving wave of his hand.

Did he know about this?

The Omega stepped up onto the platform next to me, and the temple priest cleared his throat, trying to get my attention. But I kept my eyes on my father. He simply nodded, motioning for me to continue. While I understood not wanting to end an alliance that was set in motion over two decades ago, I couldn't understand how this could be in any way acceptable to him.

Enraged, I turned and looked down at my...*mate*. Her eyes were glassy, and her bottom lip trembled.

The ceremony started, and the temple priest chanted loudly, cutting through my thoughts. He praised the Moon and the stars for binding us together, praying and swaying to a rhythmic drum. We repeated our promises to each other and our packs. The Omega spoke so quietly I could barely hear her even though I stood directly in front of her.

My anger flared with each breathy mumble that left her lips. I was meant to return to my pack with a strong partner, not a pup incapable of speaking clearly. There was no way she was of age, and her mannerisms were not those of a properly trained lady but rather a frightened pet.

She was lovely. There was no denying that. But this was unacceptable, and this deception would not stand.

The ceremony drew to a close, and a temple bishop approached the Omega with the traditional cup of tea. I glanced again at my father. His jaw was tight, and his eyes narrowed, his anger starting to surface. He didn't nod this time but didn't do anything else either, so I turned back to the Omega, preparing myself to complete the bonding.

All that was left to do was to mark her. It was required to complete the mating bite in front of witnesses to prove our union was consensual and entered into freely by both wolves. As if either one of us had a choice.

The Omega took a quick sip of the tea and choked almost immediately. She frowned and moved to hand it back, but the bishop placed his hand under the cup, forcing it back to her lips and down her throat.

She gulped the hot liquid, tears gathering in the corners of her eyes. I understood that the especially bitter tea would help dull the pain of being marked outside of mating. I had heard it could be quite painful, and my father had instructed me to be quick but precise in my movements. After all, this mark lasted for life, and the last thing I wanted was a weak scar displaying my hesitation for all to see.

Once the cup was empty, the priest instructed us to bow our heads as he said another prayer, then he motioned for me to proceed.

I sighed heavily at the sight of the pup before me. I wasn't surprised she was staring at her feet. She hadn't looked at me once throughout the entire ceremony. I let out a quick breath and tipped her chin up, her pretty face covered in silent tears.

I knew how she felt.

Brushing the dark curls away from her neck, I ran a finger over her throat, watching the vein pulse with fear. I closed my eyes to steady myself before leaning down into the crook of her neck. She smelled somewhat sweet, but it was hard to tell from the overwhelming emotions pushing off her. She needed to calm down before she gave herself a panic attack.

Not wanting to drag it out any longer, I fisted the hair at the base of her skull and jerked her body against mine, immediately sinking my teeth deep into her skin.

She stiffened and gripped my forearms, her small hands trying to steady herself. A soft whine followed by a gentle sob left her throat as my mouth flooded with her blood. I pushed my fangs in harder, tightly embedding myself into her skin, wanting the mark to be deep and dark.

I sucked hard. The metallic tang of blood melted away, and the delicate scent of spun honey washed over me. The vein in her throat pulsed against my tongue as I removed my teeth and lapped at the torn flesh, trying to soothe it.

Leaning back to look the mark over, I tipped her chin further to the side. It was deep and red against her pale skin. It was beautiful. It would probably even bruise from the force I used. My wolf was proud.

The priest clapped his hands, and loud bells within the temple rang out. The crowd outside erupted into cheers and chants, and the attendees inside stood, clapping wildly. I turned to face the excited congregation and forced a smile, taking my new mate's hand. It was cold and clammy.

Glancing down at her, I expected to see her smiling at the expressive crowd, but her face was blank and intense at the same time. She swayed, her eyes blown out, and a sheen of sweat covered her face.

There was a brief moment where I thought perhaps she might throw up, but instead, she fainted.

The Temple

Emmy

Confusion and fear swirled within me, and I slowly opened my eyes, fuzzy shapes coming into focus. My head was pounding and spinning at the same time.

The cool temple floor felt good against my cheek, and I pressed my hands flat to get my bearings. The lack of carpet told me I was on the pulpit, which explained the stab of pain in my backside. I had passed out on the hardwood.

Breathing slowly through my nose, I shifted onto my side but stopped as my eyes found my mother. She held her mouth in a tight line and spun the rings on her fingers. She looked like she wanted to hit me.

I carefully pushed myself away from her and pressed my back against the wall, not trusting myself to stand. She let out a huff and stepped away, turning to the other enraged Alphas in the room.

The crowd was gone, and all that remained was my family and the two Hund Valley wolves; my new mate and his father.

Everyone was so angry.

Their harsh scents all clashed together, sticking to the roof of my mouth and clinging to my hair. My wolf whined, too sensitive and overworked. The number of enraged Alphas I had been forced to be in the company of lately was bordering on abuse.

"This pup is not what was promised, and you fucking know it." My mate's voice pounded in my ears, and I covered them, still feeling nauseous from that horrible tea. "She looks weak and, and...how old is she? Is she even of age to provide pups?"

"Rin," my father said to the Alpha in his most diplomatic tone. "I promised you my daughter, and that is what you have."

"Where is the blonde Alpha you so thoroughly described?" Rin asked. "Because *this*," he jabbed a finger at me as if I was a piece of broken furniture, "isn't her!"

I cast my eyes down, trying to quiet my queazy stomach, but it didn't help. My throat tightened, and spit flooded my mouth. Swallowing repeatedly, I begged the Moon not to make me sick in front of all these horrible wolves. I just needed a short reprieve from their anger—just a single breath of fresh air.

"Where is the mate I was promised?" Rin growled, baring his teeth and stepping aggressively toward my father. Davon jumped between them and pushed at the Alpha's shoulders, trying to hold him back.

My stomach settled for a moment, and I realized the skin beneath my ear throbbed fiercely. I reached up to touch the tender flesh and winced as pain stabbed through my body, making the room pitch and sway.

"Don't you dare pass out," my mother spat in a low, hushed tone.

I closed my eyes, not having it in me to argue. It wasn't like I was doing this on purpose. But I was sure the embarrassment of having such a weak daughter would haunt her for the rest of her life. I hoped it kept her up at night.

"I will not let you take me for a fool!" Rin growled, shoving against Davon.

"My friends," my father said, the tremor in his voice betraying his nerves. It was so weird seeing him like this. My father backed down from no one. Ever.

Davon fought to hold back the enraged wolf, but the larger Alpha was clearly the stronger of the two, pushing my brother as he inched forward.

"Rollen! Rin!" My father's voice raised as my new mate edged closer. "I apologize for not being completely honest with you before the ceremony."

"You apologize?" Rin whispered in disbelief before letting out a vicious roar. "You apologize!"

He jerked forward, shoving my struggling brother with him. The irate Alpha wrenched free, and in a blur of movement too fast for me to truly see, he punched Davon square in the jaw. The heavy thump of his fist connecting with flesh pulsed throughout the room, then Davon hit the floor. Rin's father, Rollen, rushed forward and wrapped his arm's around his son's chest, securing the Alpha's back to his body in a vice-like hug.

Davon jumped back up, placing himself firmly between them again. His whole body shook, his wolf begging to break free, but he'd never disrespect our father that way.

"Hector," Rollen snarled. His eyes flashed red as he held his son, struggling to keep him under control. "This morning, you said that while you couldn't offer Sana to my son, your youngest daughter was more than an acceptable replacement. And I think we can all agree she's fucking not. She has no strength in her at all." He glanced at me before turning back to my father. "You had better have a *really* good excuse. Otherwise, I'm calling in my guards and ending this embarrassment once and for all."

"You knew about this?" Rin stopped struggling and turned his head to his father, his eyes wide and jaw tight.

"I was told only an hour before the ceremony, but I had not expected this." He flung a hand in my direction as he released his son.

Sucking in a determined breath as if coming to a firm decision, Rollen smoothed down the front of his dress robes, his features going dark. "Rin, get my guards."

"This morning!" My mother jumped into action. "We woke to find...we woke to find..." Her voice seemed to crack, and she suddenly stopped speaking as she buried her face in her hands. I stared at her bizarre behavior, trying to figure out what she was doing. "We lost our daughter. Our Sana is gone." She kept her face covered and let out an awful wail, pretending to cry.

It was a bold choice, but one that seemed to have worked as all the Alphas in the room instantly calmed and moved uncomfortably. My father rushed to her side, patting her back and whispering words of comfort. Davon bared his teeth at the Hund Valley wolves, who glared right back.

"Rin, I truly am sorry," my father said, his demeanor suddenly sad and quiet. "Our intention was never to deceive you, but it's true. Our Sana is gone."

"This is bullshit!" Rin yelled. "You expect me to believe that the young she-wolf I just saw yesterday died suddenly in the middle of the night?" He stepped right up to my father, his body vibrating with an intense rage. "If this is a trick, I swear to the Moon and stars, I will fucking end you."

My father held his hands up in surrender, and my eyes

went wide at the gesture. I had never seen him bow out of a fight. He always welcomed a challenge, meeting anyone willing to throw fists head-on.

"This isn't a trick. I assure you. Please, friend. Listen to me," he said with fake, sad eyes. "Take Emmy. I know she doesn't have the beauty or education Sana did, but she does have her good qualities. She is a good Omega, and she will be good for you and Hund Valley."

I looked at my hands, wishing the floor would swallow me up. I was used to my parents' general disappointment in my simple existence, but they didn't usually flaunt it in front of others.

"It's true," my brother said. "Emmy is very kind and sweet, and she is a very obedient Omega. I am sure you will find happiness with her."

I hated all of them.

I hated my parents, brother, new mate, and even myself. If I had been born anything other than an Omega, I would have had some worth to my family—strength and cunning. Something to be respected. But instead, I was weak; my only purpose to provide young for the strong.

I was a commodity to be traded, but even my new mate didn't want me.

"How old is she?" Rin asked forcefully, speaking as if I wasn't in the room.

"I am not yet of age," I said before my parents could lie again. My voice was low and strained, but I knew they all heard me. My mother's eyes cut at me, violence flashing behind them, but I didn't care anymore. Sana wasn't dead, and I wasn't twenty yet. That was the truth.

"You made me mark a fucking pup?" Rin recoiled, disgust clouding his handsome features. He squared his shoulders and tightened his fists so hard I could practically see his fingernails digging into his skin.

"This is unforgivable." His voice was loud and hard, and it sliced through me, making my spine ache and wolf bellow.

Maybe Andrus would have been a better choice after all.

"But she will be of age by the end of the next full moon," my father assured quickly. "That's only a few weeks away. This is still a good match."

"Alpha Rin," my mother rushed toward him, her eyes brimming with panic.

I knew what she was thinking. If he rejected me now, it would be catastrophic for them. The shame would open them up to stronger, more powerful Alphas to challenge my father for the position of Pack Alpha. And the old wolf didn't have the strength to protect what was his anymore.

"I assure you." Her words shook as they rushed out of her, bursting with actual emotion this time. "Emmy will be a good mate. I apologize for not having her trained properly, but we honestly never thought this could have happened. The grief of losing our beautiful Sana was just too much and, and..." she bowed her head, pretending to cry again.

I stared at her and her stupid game, not bothering to hide my contempt. She was going to hand me over to this unhinged beast to save her own skin.

"I should rip you all apart," Rin growled, eyeing both my parents, then my brother, making his threat known and felt.

"Do what you must," Davon said simply, still holding his head high. "But Emmy is all we have to offer you."

Silence stretched out as no one moved or spoke. I tried to keep my attention on the fuming Alphas around me as they decided whether or not to kill each other, but the ache in my body kept demanding my focus. My neck throbbed, and my wolf whimpered. This was all too much.

"I leave this up to you, son. Take her or leave her," Rollen said a little too casually for my liking. "I leave our pack's future to you." He crossed his arms and glared at my father.

Rin stepped back, really looking at me for the first time since the ceremony. Everyone seemed to turn with him, their eyes making my skin crawl. My dress was suddenly too tight, and I found it a little hard to breathe, my lungs unable to get a proper fill of air.

Rin's fierce eyes cut right through me. Then his chest deflated a bit. "Let's go," he said, his mouth etched with anger.

I stayed on the floor, not knowing what to do. Was he saying that he and his kin were leaving without me? Or was he telling me to go with them?

I stared up at him dumbly.

"Get up," he snapped, making me jump.

I pulled myself to my feet, my head spinning, then crossed my arms over my chest. I expected him to yell at me again, but he remained silent, just watching me.

My mother let out a soft sigh of relief, giving me an approving smile.

A wave of sizzling anger burned through my veins. All the stupid power in this room and every one of them was only interested in throwing abuse at me, the only one with no choice.

They could all go to hell for all I cared.

"I will not tell you again." Rin's voice was gruff and deliberate as he looked at me with dark, hard eyes. "Go!"

My feet moved at his command. I made sure to circle widely around my parents. I didn't want either one of them to have the chance to make a scene or pretend to miss me.

Marching past Rin and his father, I moved as fast as I could toward the back door, where a carriage waited to take us to Hund Valley. The ceremony dictated that the mate was to enter the front of the temple, a member of the Casin Pack, and leave out the back, destined for their new home.

I threw open the door, causing a few Hund Valley guards to startle. They jumped to attention as I wrenched open the carriage door and shoved myself inside, bunching my dress up in my fists.

My new mate slowly followed, stepping out of the temple and stopping next to the carriage. He glanced at his father briefly, a look of uncertainty on his face, before turning back to me.

"Do you want to say goodbye to your family?" he asked. His tone was harsh despite what I assumed was supposed to be a kind offer.

I shook my head, refusing to look at any of them.

Davon came into view, his big body taking up the entire doorway to the temple. He had a soft look in his eyes, just watching me. I jerked my head away. My life with them was over.

Rin climbed inside the small carriage and settled across from me. He gave a quick nod, and we lurched forward. The guards outside the little windows picked up their pace and walked protectively next to us.

My eyes moved over every inch of the village, trying to memorize every cabin and tree and flower. It was probably the last time I'd ever see Casin again. My wolf whined, and I blinked back a few tears, already missing the only home I had ever known.

My eyes drifted across the crowd of happy faces. They all cheered and sang, celebrating the sealed alliance and continued peace between our packs. A few pups ran up along the carriage, squealing and laughing, and I smiled back at them, not having it in me to steal their joy.

The carriage rolled on, and I looked over the town square one more time.

My eyes instantly fell on the one face that wasn't beaming with joy.

Andrus glowered, and his grey eyes bore straight into mine. He slowly opened his mouth, and his lips moved as if saying something, but his words died within the bustle of the crowd. It made me shiver.

My disaster of a bonding to an irate Alpha, blessed by the unheard words of the most terrifying wolf I'd ever met.

I let out a shuddering breath and wondered what I had done to anger the Moon so thoroughly.

The Carriage

Rin

THE PUP—*MY mate*—cried all afternoon. Her lips trembled, and she occasionally let out a soft sob, but for the most part, she barely made a sound. Just continually wiping at her cheeks and chin, drying her hands on her dress.

It was all so fucking uncomfortable.

What the hell was I supposed to do with her?

I couldn't properly mate her. It was beneath me to think of a pup in such a manner, even if her coming of age was only a few weeks away. And she had no real education to speak of. I couldn't let her interact with other pack leaders or expect her to know how to behave should the Were-King choose to extend an invitation. And, as an Omega, she was susceptible to others manipulating her with their Alpha-voice.

This was a fucking disaster, and I couldn't let anyone find out. It would make my father and me look weak to allow such a feeble pack to deceive us thoroughly.

Fucking Hector.

As dusk settled, the Omega finally fell asleep. It was a relief to have a few moments of silence that weren't punctuated with sniffles and muffled sobs.

Her head rolled gently toward me as the carriage moved over the rough terrain, and I could finally look at her properly. She was pretty—soft features and pouty lips. Her rosy cheeks had streaks from her tears washing away, what I assumed was some kind of paint. And her hands still gripped the fabric of her dress hard, even as soft snores left her lips.

My eyes fell to a bruise on her arm just above her wrist. It looked fresh and not yet at its darkest shade. My wolf growled at the sight, not caring for the idea of someone touching something that was mine in such a severe manner.

While I hadn't exactly been kind to the Omega, there was no excuse for handling one so roughly. They were soft and fragile creatures, not built for harsh discipline or violence. And, while I was still very fucking angry about it, she was mine now, and no one fucking touches what's mine.

I turned my attention to the passing mountains in the distance. There was nothing I could do about old bruises now. I'd just have to be mindful should her family choose to visit. I leaned back, taking advantage of the quiet journey, and allowed myself to fall asleep.

"Sir," my personal guard, Zev, said as he opened the carriage door, jerking me awake. "We've arrived at the camp."

"Thank you, Commander," I said, stepping out into the fresh air. I arched my back and rolled my shoulders, trying to relieve the stiffness that had settled in my joints.

I hated riding in carriages, but I didn't want to disrespect Casin's traditions. Although looking at the still sleeping

Omega, I doubted she would have cared if we had followed her pack's customs or not.

The Moon shone beautifully, gifting us with her joyous light. Under any other circumstances, I would have sworn the skies were blessing us, but not today, not after that disastrous ceremony.

A maiden bowed lowly to me before walking past to wake the Omega and prepare her for the evening.

Zev stood at attention, waiting patiently for my next orders.

"Walk with me," I said, moving through the tents.

The camp was prepared while my father and I continued to Casin. Its purpose was to allow me and my mate to complete our mating rituals and finalize our bonding. But that would *not* be happening. Not with a pup.

I stepped inside the luxurious tent prepared for me. It was large, comfortable, and illuminated by the soft glow of several lanterns. A plush pallet laid on the carpeted ground, and a spread of various fruits, dried meats, and wine was provided.

"Hector fucked us," I said, turning to face Zev once he closed the tent's entrance. He stiffened at my words but waited for me to continue. "They forced a fucking child on me, not the Alpha my family was promised."

"A child?" He tilted his head slightly.

"Literally a pup." I slumped into a chair. "She won't be of age until the end of the next full Moon. Which I understand is only a few weeks away but still." I jerked at the belts around my middle, fury consuming me all over again. "And she's a fucking Omega! I'm not good with Omegas. They're emotional and irrational and beyond reason."

I could see Zev fighting a smile. I knew he was thinking of my younger brother, who I adored, but still struggled daily to find common ground.

"Shut up," I snapped at his annoying expression. He broke out into a wide grin, irritating me even more. "This is serious."

Zev cleared his throat, and his face instantly fell to his usual professional demeanor. "Sir," he said, meeting my eyes. "I'm assuming since you took her, you intend to mate her?"

"I can't fucking do that, Zev. She's a pup."

"Does anyone other than yourself and your father know about her age? About her not being the mate that was expected?"

I sighed, rubbing my face hard. "No one outside of Casin and my father. To our pack, she is what was promised."

"Then I would suggest not sharing that information with anyone. After the next full Moon, you can proceed with her as planned. The alliance still sealed and an heir provided," he said calmly.

In addition to being the commander of my family's personal guards, he was also my best friend. He was smart, level-headed, and almost always right—not that I'd ever admit it.

"Let everyone think she's of age," Zev continued. "I think it would be best to keep this embarrassment a secret. It wouldn't look good for others to think you could be so easily tricked or willing to let such behavior slide."

"I should have killed them all," I growled. It would have made my life so much easier. Even if Casin's location kept the population of orcs and goblins under control—protecting all wolves from the violent creatures—but I'd be willing to risk all of Havre falling to the bastards if it meant putting Hector in his fucking place.

"Why didn't you?" Zev cocked a brow. He was the only Alpha in all of Havre that I would ever allow to ask me such a question.

"At that moment, it seemed stupid to start a war over

something as trivial as a fucked up mating ceremony. I didn't think it was fair to sacrifice the lives of my men for a missing mate, especially since a replacement had been provided. But now..." I sighed, regretting my every decision. "I should have ripped Hector's throat out."

The entrance to the tent fluttered, then slowly pulled open. The Omega peeked her head in, glancing at me, then Zev. He stepped forward and grabbed the edge of the tent flap, pulling it to the side so she could enter. Keeping her eyes cast down, she stepped inside.

She wore a white nightdress, and her hair was straight, the wild curls from the ceremony washed out. The traditional, deep blue paint adorned her arms and peeked out beneath the hem of her short bedclothes. Swirls and stars across her stomach and thighs.

My eyes drifted over her form, finding her dark nipples straining against the thin material. Her tits were much less than I'd prefer, but the stiff peaks still made my dick plump a bit.

I groaned and pinched the bridge of my nose.

"My Lady." Zev gave her a deep bow before introducing himself. "Please, let me know if there is anything you need."

She barely nodded, not quite meeting Zev's eyes. He cut me a quick glance, a smirk on his annoying face, then ducked out of the tent, leaving us alone.

It was hard to look at the Omega and not think of how I'd been so thoroughly fooled. My blood boiled, and I pressed my lips together to keep from snarling. Scaring the frightened Omega further wouldn't fix anything and would only add to my already substantial problems.

"Emyanna—"

"Emmy," she interrupted, then immediately winced. I could smell the fear rolling off her trembling shoulders.

I sighed and stood up, removing my robes. She shied away from me as if expecting me to pounce on her. She was so small and scared, and after seeing the way her family threw her away so easily, I couldn't help but feel bad for the pup.

What the fuck was I supposed to do with her?

The Camp

Emmy

I AWOKE to a gentle voice and was briefly startled to find myself sitting in a carriage. I had hoped it had all been a dream.

"Omega Emyanna," a young Beta with honey-colored hair set in tight curls whispered gently. "Please follow me, My Lady."

She was so beautiful, with soft skin, dark eyes, and perfectly carved features. She looked like a doll, and I couldn't help but stare.

The Beta gently took my hand and led me away from the carriage.

My eyes moved all around the large meadow behind us. Several tents and lots of loud, rowdy Alphas filled the flat land. There must have been at least forty or so wolves in total, and the sight was a bit overwhelming. Fires dotted the campsite, and wolves sang, laughed, and wrestled with onlookers cheering and clapping. The atmosphere was generally happy, but it still made my wolf nervous.

"My name is Dara, My Lady," the Beta said as we moved further away from the camp and into the woods. A trail illuminated by lanterns gave the forest a magical glow as we walked toward a shimmering lake. "I'll be your personal maid. So please, let me know if there's anything you need."

I nodded, noticing two other wolves behind us; a tall, demanding female Alpha with light brown hair in a tight braid and a shorter, softer-looking wolf with blonde hair and round cheeks. I stopped, stunned, and turned to look at him.

"You're an Omega," I said. It was stupid and obvious, but I couldn't help it. He was wearing the same deep blue robes as the other guards, clearly one of them.

"Yes, ma'am," he said, bowing his head.

"Are you...are you a guard?"

"No, ma'am," he smiled. "I'm a valet for the guards. I help take care of them," he added when he realized I didn't know what that meant.

"Are you the only Omega on staff, or are there others?"

He glanced at Dara, who smiled and nodded. "There are others, ma'am," he said more confidently. "In the kitchens and gardens, all over really."

"Omegas are allowed to work?" I spun, asking Dara.

"Yes, My Lady," she smiled. "Omegas are permitted to work until they are mated and have young. Then I believe it just becomes too difficult, but some still choose to work in the nurseries or schools."

I couldn't believe it. A pack that allowed Omegas to leave their homes and be of use. I couldn't stop the large grin that pulled at my cheeks and made me want to laugh out loud. There was a real possibility that I was going to a village that wouldn't hate me based purely on my status.

Dara giggled at my reaction before gently pulling me

forward again. "Do Omegas not work in your pack?" she asked as the edge of the small lake came into view.

"Omegas aren't allowed to do much of anything in my village," I mumbled to myself.

I wanted to tell her Omegas were seen as weak and burdensome, but I was bursting with too much excitement for the young male Omega removing the flowers from my hair. Pride bubbling out of my chest for him.

I continued to smile as Dara carefully removed my makeup, rubbing a soft cloth over my cheeks and lips. I couldn't remember being so relaxed and happy. Sana always brought me happiness. But she had been so upset lately, keeping herself locked away and leaving me to fend for myself.

"I know new mates are sometimes in the dark about what is expected when it comes to bonding for the first time," Dara said sweetly, untying the laces of my corset. "Do you have any questions about tonight?"

The excitement in my chest faded, and I looked down at my feet. "No," I whispered, my cheeks burning.

I had a million questions. One of them being, *how do I get out of this?* But I didn't expect anyone to be able to answer that.

I was just going to do as my mother said and do whatever my mate wanted. Even with my limited knowledge of mating, I doubted knowing anything more would help.

Dara washed me thoroughly in the cool lake before applying rosewater to my skin and some kind of sweet oil to my hair. It made me feel light and pretty. She brushed out my tangles and painted my stomach, legs, and arms with deep blue swirls, stars, and flowers that contrasted wildly against my pale skin.

The female Alpha, Ravana, kept watch, making sure no one wandered near the lake. And the young Omega, Karlin, dutifully cleaned up, folding my dress and putting away the little pots of paint.

I pulled on the white nightdress provided and nothing else. When I asked for some underwear, Dara smiled and said that any other garments wouldn't be necessary. I could feel my cheeks burn as I nodded in understanding.

"Come, My Lady," Dara said, holding out a hand.

She led me to a large tent situated on the edge of the camp, away from the rest of the wolves. Guards stood in a circle-like formation not too far off, obviously meant to protect and give a certain amount of privacy. It made me nervous, knowing someone might overhear whatever was about to happen.

"My Lady," Dara said as Ravana and Karlin bowed, then left, disappearing into the little tents in the center of the camp. She looked around, then leaned into my ear, whispering, "Have Alpha Rin clean your mark a little more properly. It's not been done well."

I reached up to touch my neck, but she grabbed my hand.

"Let him do it," she whispered. She gave me a sweet smile and a quick squeeze of my hands before leaving me alone in front of the tent.

I stared at the heavy fabric of the entrance, trying to force myself to move. My heart was thumping hard in my throat, and my wolf whimpered at the thought of being so close to the angry Alpha once again.

A seemingly tense conversation within the tent drifted toward me, and I let my hand hang in the air for a moment, too scared to enter.

But I knew it couldn't be helped, so I gripped the heavy tent flap, and pulled hard.

Rin sat in a chair, looking very serious, as he talked to a very tall Alpha with short black hair. They both turned toward me, and the tall Alpha pulled at the edge of the tent's entrance, letting me in.

"My Lady," the tall Alpha smiled. It lit his whole face up. His dark eyes were warm and soft, and I could see the faintest ring of purple around the edge of his irises. He looked magical. "I'm Commander Zev. I am here to protect and serve you. Please, let me know if there is anything you need." He bowed to both me and Rin, then disappeared, leaving me alone with my scary mate.

I stood in the same spot, feeling Rin's eyes roam over me as I stared intensely at the floor. He lounged in the chair with his legs spread wide, taking up so much room in the tight space. I felt so small.

"Emyanna—"

"Emmy," I corrected him, then winced. Squeezing my hands together, I waited for him to yell or hit me. But he did neither.

He sighed deeply, then stood. He pulled off his robes and flung them over the chair, moving around the tent and grabbing a carafe of what looked like wine. "Did you tell anyone that you aren't of age?"

My brows pulled together, trying to figure out what he meant. Of course, people knew. My whole pack back home knew.

"Your maid," he practically yelled when I didn't answer, speaking as if I were stupid. "Did you tell your maid, just now, how old you are?"

I shook my head, my wolf bristling and whimpering at the same time.

"Good," he spat. "Don't tell anyone. Ever. Do you understand?"

I nodded quickly.

"Do you understand?" he asked again, his expression darkening. His anger gripped me unexpectedly, and I struggled to find my words for a moment.

"Yes," I forced out. I wanted my voice to come out strong and loud, matching his intensity, but I sounded just as weak as I felt.

"Your father took me for a fool, forcing you on me," he poured himself a drink, downing it in one go, "and I let him."

He shook his head and pushed a slow growl into the air. "As far as Hund Valley and the rest of my family are concerned, you are of age from this moment on." He turned to face me. "Is that clear?"

I nodded, mumbling a quick response and throwing him what I hoped was a scowl but was probably more of a pout. None of this was my fault. I didn't deserve his anger.

"Good."

He tugged at his shirt, pulling it off in one swift motion. A chill danced over my skin, despite the warm summer night, and I fought against the urge to back away. Not seeming to notice my unease, he jerked down his pants, leaving himself in only his snug undergarments.

His toned muscles moved under his tan skin as he grabbed a few blankets folded neatly in the corner. His strong arms flexed as he spread the quilts over a pallet in the center of the room. My eyes drifted to a thin strip of dark hair that trailed under his belly button, disappearing beneath his waistband.

I pressed my knees together as an almost icky sensation burned in the pit of my stomach. My wolf shivered, fear and longing mixing together. This Alpha was our mate, the bite on my neck pulsing with his rage, but he was still a stranger. His emotions completely foreign to me.

Twisting my hands together, I waited for him to tell me what to do, not taking my eyes off the pallet on the floor. It seemed to grow bigger, consuming the whole space and demanding my attention.

"You don't have to look so terrified," he said, settling

himself on the blankets. "I won't touch you. I have no interest in corrupting pups."

Rejection burned my eyes, and I swallowed down a firm lump in my throat. I should be relieved, but it only scared me more.

Why did he bring me here if he had no intention of claiming me? Was he going to abandon me in the woods? Give me to someone else? Kill me?

"I'm sure you're tired," he said, snapping me to attention. "Lay down. Sleep."

My feet pulled me forward at his command, and I sat on the edge of the bed, nerves pricking my skin.

"Alpha," I whispered.

He didn't move, laying on his back with one arm tucked behind his head.

"Alpha," I said a little louder.

He cracked his eyes open and looked at me. "What?" he asked, clearly annoyed.

"My mark," I whispered, hovering a hand over my neck. "It needs... it's not...."

I thought about not bringing it up at all, but a dirty mating bite would mean infection and possibly death. I had no choice.

Rin sat up and startled me by pulling me to him by my arm. He wasn't necessarily rough, but it scared me just the same. Without a word, he tilted my chin up to better view the bite. My hands gripped at the hem of my nightdress, and I jerked when I realized I had smeared the designs on my legs.

"The paint," I gasped.

"Ignore it," he said as he moved my head around, examining the wound. "It's meant to make a mess." He ran his thumb around my sensitive skin, his breath fanning over my throat. "I did a poor job of cleaning this. I apologize."

Before I could respond, he leaned into me and pressed his

lips firmly to my neck. It stung as he sucked and lapped softly at my raw skin, easing the pain away. His strong arms wrapped around my middle, holding me closer as he worked me over.

Out of nowhere, my chest squeezed with the same fear from when Andrus attacked me in my bedroom. Rin said he had no interest in taking me, but what if he changed his mind? Would he force me like Andrus did? Would he hurt me? Would he care if I cried?

Why was this all so scary and confusing?

Unsure of what to do with my hands, I finally rested them on his shoulders. I let out a slow, uneasy breath and tried to relax, focusing on the warmth radiating from the Alpha.

He moved his large hands up my back, cradling my head gently. For a brief moment, I felt caged, but it fell away almost instantly, giving me comfort. I felt...safe.

Rin moved his lips gently around the edges of my mark, sucking and kissing. A sweet swipe of his tongue moved just beneath my ear, and a deep rumble left his chest.

The knot in my stomach uncurled as the room filled with the Alpha's intoxicating warmth, and the icky sensation deep within me melted into something...*more*. Something that burned and twisted in a horribly wonderful way.

My wolf purred.

He smelled so good, like spring water and cedar and rain. It was indescribable, and I inhaled deeply, the softest sigh leaving my lips.

His body stiffened, and he stopped his movements.

Rin leaned his head back slowly, looking down into my flushed face. His dark eyes danced over my features before settling on my lips. He was so close, his breath fanning across my cheeks and mouth.

His throat worked as he swallowed thickly. "Better?" His voice was deep and husky.

"Yes," I whispered, unable to look away. There was something comforting in his eyes that my wolf adored, even if his harsh tone did set me on edge.

"Good." He immediately removed himself from my body and rolled over, facing away from me. "Go to sleep."

The Tent

Rin

I OPENED my eyes to see the Omega fast asleep and clinging to my side, her soft thigh thrown over my stomach. The thin material of her nightdress pulled up in her sleep, exposing the curve of her backside. I looked away and gently rolled her off of me. Grabbing the blanket, I flung it over her body, not letting myself look back at her.

Rubbing my face hard, I stared at the deep blue canvas of the tent. Last night, while cleaning my bite, there was a moment my wolf threatened to take over. The urge to claim the Omega, rough and hard, was so overpowering it shocked me and took all my strength to stay in control.

I needed to get ahold of my instincts. Just because my wolf didn't care about age didn't mean I'd fall victim to his desires. I was in charge of my beast, not the other way around.

Grabbing my pants, I reminded myself that my pull to the Omega was simply a side effect of the mating bite and that I had more than enough self-control to keep from lusting after a pup. I fastened my belt, trying to ignore the throb in my groin that mocked me, proving otherwise.

The Omega—my mate—was simply the final knot in a long-standing alliance. Of course, she would provide an heir, as was expected, but that's all this was. And until she became of age and received proper training, she was nothing more than a burden, in need of constant supervision and a decent education.

"Alpha?"

I turned to the Omega's small voice. She sat in the center of the pallet and rubbed her eyes with the back of her hand. Blue paint smeared over most of her body, including one cheek and the tip of her nose. I pressed my lips together to suppress a smile.

"Sir?" Zev's voice cut through the soft silence of the morning. "Are you awake?"

I raised my eyes to the Omega, and she quickly covered herself with the blanket, pulling it tightly around her shoulders before nodding. "Yes," I said once she settled.

Zev entered and bowed to me, then to the Omega. "Good morning," he smiled. "I hope your night went well."

I nodded.

"We have several things to discuss this morning, Sir. But..." his voice trailed off as he looked me over.

"What?" I asked, looking down at my exposed chest.

"Sir," Zev stepped toward me and leaned into my ear. "Given that the bonding ritual was completed last night, I would have expected you to have more paint on you." He stepped back, giving me a knowing look.

I couldn't help but agree. Blue paint-covered one arm and a spot on my stomach from where she had slept pushed against me, but other than that, I was mostly clean.

"I'll be out shortly," I excused him.

Zev bowed again, then left.

"Omega." I crossed the tent and sat next to her feet.

She looked nervous. All Omegas always looked nervous. By now, I just assumed it was their default state. "I need to smear some of your paint on me."

"Is it not dry?" She rubbed her fingertips over her forearm.

"It's mixed with animal fat, so it stays greasy," I assured. "Just...rub your arm, here." I patted my chest. She lifted her arm, then hesitated, her wide eyes not quite meeting mine. "I'm not going to bite you," I said, much harsher than intended.

She gave a slight nod of her head, then did as she was told, moving the back of her forearm over my pecs, occasionally looking up at me with questioning eyes.

She worked the slick, blue substance over my other arm and shoulders while I tried to smear what I could down my abs. She shifted, exposing her thighs caked in thick streaks of paint. Without thinking, I reached out and pushed my hands through the mess, squeezing her soft flesh in the process.

She jerked back, her bottom lip already trembling.

I held my hands up in surrender and opened my mouth to apologize but stopped. Only weak Alphas acted in ways that warranted apologies, and I hadn't meant to grab her. Surely she understood that.

"Why are we doing this?" she asked quietly, wide eyes watching my every movement.

"The paint proves you were touched and claimed. It reassures the pack that our bond has been blessed under the stars and hopefully honored with an heir."

Her brow twisted and she pressed her sticky hands together, slowly pulling them apart over and over again. It seemed as if she wasn't aware she was doing it.

Feeling her confusion, I added, "It's a part of the mating ritual in my pack."

"Will people want to...look at me?" she asked. Her hands clasped together tight. "To see if my paint is smeared?"

"No," I said quickly. I had seen more than enough of her tears yesterday, and I was in no hurry to see them again. "Your maid will come and clean you up, then report to the priests that I did my job. I, however, will walk around without a shirt, covered in paint all day." I couldn't help but smirk at the surprised look on her face. "It's tradition."

"Okay," she said, seeming to relax. She looked me over, then reached out and dragged her sticky hand down my side. I stiffened when her fingers ran over my ribs just beneath my arm.

"I'm sorry." She jerked her hand back. "Did that hurt?"

"No," I snorted. "It just...tickled a bit."

A smile curved her lips, and her face lit up. A gentle laugh left her throat, and I couldn't help but smile at her reaction.

The silly things Omegas found entertaining.

After a few more minutes of rubbing and smearing, we deemed ourselves messy enough. I stepped away from her and reached for the tent flap.

"Alpha! Wait."

She hurried forward, stopping directly in front of me. She stood, shifting from foot to foot, nervous energy radiating off of her. After a moment's hesitation, she finally reached a blue hand up to my face. Her fingers brushed against my jaw before pressing firmly against my cheek. Her movements were cautious and deliberate, as if in the presence of a dangerous animal.

"Okay," she whispered, backing up and turning her eyes to her feet. "All done."

I gave her a curt nod then stepped out to start my day. Zev stood just outside, alert and ready. His eyes widened when he saw me, and he smiled.

"What's the report from the patrols?" I asked, walking briskly toward the camp.

"A few of our scouts spotted some rogues last night, coming from the direction of Casin, but we were able to chase them off. No injuries. No other incidents. Fairly quiet night for the most part."

We walked through the camp to check over the men. I stopped and spoke with the guards, valets, and maids, ensuring there were no issues and we were on track to leave for the day. Then I moved on to the scouts.

"Trouble last night?" I asked, stepping up to Captain Dell.

He and the scouts he commanded all stopped eating, giving me a quick bow of their heads. I preferred my men to forego full formal greetings outside the village in case we were followed by anyone interested in targeting a high-statused Alpha. It also allowed me to be a little closer with my brothers in, what could be, very dangerous situations.

You don't want a warrior concerned with courtesies when they should be tracking threats.

"We found a band of about five rogues on our trail." Captain Dell waved a young Alpha over. She rushed to him, eager energy in her every movement.

"Fawn," he clapped the she-wolf on the shoulder, "was able to take one down before we chased off the others."

I immediately shook her hand, thanking her for her good work. She smiled wide, pride pouring off her strong shoulders.

"Did he give you a good fight?" I smirked, noticing her skin held not even a single scratch.

She cocked a grin and snorted. "Barely, Sir."

I laughed, exchanged a few more pleasantries with the other men, then pulled Dell away so they could finish eating.

"Do you think they were hoping for supplies, or did they seem to have a purpose?"

"I'm not sure," he answered. "They had all the markings of

genuine rogues, branding on their necks, dirty clothes, and a bit on the thin side. But I'm not dumb enough to ignore the threat."

"Rightfully so." Zev gave a quick nod.

"Please let me or Commander Zev know if you catch any scent or see any trace of them."

"Of course, Sir." Dell gave me a quick nod, and I dismissed him back to his meal.

The whole situation made me uneasy. This wouldn't be an issue if it were only my men and me, but we had service Betas, a few Valet Omegas, and my mate in tow. It was too serious a situation to ignore.

Turning back to the camp, I stifled a groan. I still needed to give a full report to my father. Zev clapped me on the back in a reassuring manner as we approached his tent.

Thankfully the meeting with him was quick. I made sure he saw my painted skin, and he smiled in approval, happy the alliance was completed and sealed. I filled him in on the scouts and the status of the remainder of the camp. Then he waved me off.

I motioned for Zev to follow me toward a few hunters preparing to head out. Our group was rather large, and a few more kills were needed to feed the last of the men.

Once we hit the treeline, I shifted. Bones and muscle glided into place, my true form taking control. Then I broke into a full sprint.

We needed to be quick in our hunt. Staying in one spot for too long invited the attention of possibly more rogues and scavengers. But more importantly, I needed to clear my mind and lungs of the Omega's sweet scent. It clung to me, making everything else seem almost dull and less important.

It was an odd sensation, and I didn't fucking care for it.

The Next Morning
◠◡◠

Emmy

I GORGED myself on the fruit and nuts left out from the night before. I hadn't eaten properly in the last few days and was starving. After breakfast, I busied myself by building a small nest in the center of the pallet. My nerves were shot, and the tight pull of the soft fabric around my shoulders settled my wolf.

The thickest quilt smelled like Rin, and I found myself nuzzling it as I grew bored. There wasn't much to do in the small space, and my mind quickly drifted.

I wondered what my mate was doing.

Groaning, I picked at a loose thread on the blanket, wishing I had something to read. An image of the tiny, yellow book Andrus pulled from his belt lingered in my mind, and I shuttered, hugging my knees to my chest.

Rin might not be the Alpha I had always dreamed of, but he was infinitely better than Andrus, even if he was mean and scared the breath out of me most of the time. Rin didn't give me the creepy feeling Andrus did.

At least I didn't have to worry about Sana. She was no longer caged in Casin. I wanted to believe she was free, running through the mountains with the wind in her hair and dirt at her feet. She deserved happiness, and while a part of me hated her for leaving me, I still loved and missed her dearly. Even though she should be here instead of me, I couldn't condemn her for escaping a life I didn't want either.

Dara arrived around mid-morning, and I couldn't have been happier. The sticky paint was starting to make my skin itch, and I was ready to be clean. It took the rest of the morning for the two of us to wash the gooey mess off, but Dara made the difficult task rather enjoyable.

She told me wonderful stories of her family and Hund Valley's various traditions and rituals each year. I smiled as it all played to my imagination. The very idea of attending festivals and seeing the beautiful land she described so perfectly made my heart ready to burst.

The only thing that dimmed my mood was the thought of spending so much time with Rin. His expression was pinched, his tone too sharp, and his aggressive mannerisms set me on edge. But I knew once we got to Hund Valley, he'd spend most of his time performing his duties, and I would barely have to see him, or at least I hoped. After all, my parents rarely stood in the same room together.

Dara secured a beautifully stitched sash around my middle, holding my new blue robes in place. She tied it into a perfect bow, then set to work on the smaller, more delicate ribbons that ran up the length of my forearms, creating a snug fit. The whole outfit flared over my waist and twirled over the short, fitted trousers when I spun. I simply loved it.

"Would you like to head down to the lake so you can properly wash?" she asked.

I glanced down at my completely clothed body, not under-standing why I'd need to bathe. We just scrubbed every inch of me clean and spent a good fifteen minutes getting me dressed.

"I think I'm okay," I said, feeling that there was something more she was trying to say.

Dara smiled before leaning in and whispering, "I've heard it can help to sit in cool water after mating for the first time."

My face burned, and I nodded, not wanting her to know the shameful truth. My mate had rejected me. Even though I was deeply grateful to him for not forcing himself on me, it hurt.

Between my wolf, my mind, and my heart, I was so confused.

"That would be nice," I mumbled, unable to meet her eyes. What would she think of me if she knew the truth? I couldn't even tempt my own mate. I was useless.

She took my hand, and we walked through what was left of the camp.

Most of the tents and supplies were packed up and loaded onto a large, horse-drawn cart. An intricately decorated carriage I didn't recognize pulled my attention. It rolled off into the forest with half the guards going with it. I turned to Dara, scared we were being left behind.

"The pack leader, Alpha Rollen, is leaving before us this morning," she said, noticing the panic on my face. "He's eager to get home."

I nodded but turned to look for the simple carriage I had ridden in yesterday, not relaxing until I found it. Two Betas were busy brushing the horses while the animals ate, not looking to be in any hurry to leave. I exhaled, relieved, and turned my attention to the chilly lake in the distance. Prepared to sit in it to hide my shame.

THE JOURNEY WASN'T AS bad as I had expected. I would even say it was kind of exciting.

We moved at a steady pace, only stopping to eat or sleep under the stars. Dara explained that it took too long to set up camp, and now that the ritual bonding was complete, it was essential to move quickly to get home. The journey would take almost two weeks, and I could tell the guards were growing anxious from being away from their village for so long.

Zev let me roam a bit with Dara during our short breaks, and the freedom was exhilarating, even though he insisted on following us. I was sure Rin had ordered him to stick to me like honey, but I didn't mind. Zev had a calming presence for an Alpha, and he smiled a lot.

I hardly saw my mate, though. Rin walked near me only a handful of times over the course of the week, and he rarely spoke to me. Always leaving after only a few moments, his eyes barely even flickering in my direction. It was a relief not to have to put up with his aggressive presence and lingering scent, which, after much thought, I decided I didn't like.

An icy tingle pricked my cheeks, and I watched in awe as the air around us shifted into a hazy frost, biting into the summer heat. I shivered and wrapped my arms over my chest, my robes not providing near enough warmth.

"My Lady," Zev said, suddenly at my side and holding out a thick shaw. I glanced around at the other wolves, all seemingly unaffected by the drop in temperature. I considered declining it, but the chill that ran up my spine won me over.

"My apologies," he said. "There's a cluster of kunzite crystals under the ground in this area. We should be through it shortly."

Massive, pink crystals dotted the land, cutting out of the ground, slicing into trees, and pushing against large rocks. The air was so calm and clean, and I savored it despite the cold. I brushed my fingertips over the point of a pink stone and jerked back. A fierce chill sliced through my arm, pinching at my nerves and joints.

"Careful, My Lady," Dara said, wrapping an arm around my shoulders. "We're almost through."

The air slowly warmed, and the summer wind swirled, fighting off the chill. The crystals became more sparse before all together disappearing, and my cheeks tingled as warmth filled me once again.

After traveling a good distance for the day, we settled into a plush, grassy meadow for the night. My feet were killing me, and I was ready for a proper bed.

I pulled at Dara's middle and snuggled into her beautiful, floral scent. My body melted into the soft earth as I watched a few of the scouts shift into their wolves and disappear into the forest before sleep took me.

THE SHARP YIP of an injured wolf cut through my dreams, and I snapped my eyes open. The guards around us were up and standing at the ready—a few shifting into their wolves. Rin paced along the meadow's border, yelling into the darkness within the treeline, but I couldn't hear what he was saying.

"My Lady. Come," Zev ordered, suddenly standing over me.

I froze, looking up at his massive form in shock. Dara hitched her hands under my arms and heaved me up, forcing me to my feet. Zev grabbed my wrist and pulled me into the trees away from Rin and the guards, Dara quick at our heels.

We ran forever, not stopping until we came to a few massive rocks pressed into a hillside. Zev guided me onto the ground, pushing my back against the cool stone. Dara moved to sit directly in front of me, her arms out in a protective manner and her eyes scanning the trees around us. It was as if they knew exactly what to do, and it scared me even more.

I watched Zev pace, his eyes darting toward every little sound.

"Why aren't we with the others?" I whispered as quietly as I could in Dara's ear.

"It's safer if you aren't near the fight should someone attack." Her eyes continuously moved over the dark forest. "Alphas aren't always careful with Omegas when in their wolf-form."

I pressed myself into her back, my chin on her shoulder. "Thank you."

Dara pulled her attention away from the trees and turned her head to look at me. "It's an honor to help protect our pack's future Luna," she whispered sweetly.

I returned her smile but stiffened at her words. I hadn't thought about what mating Rin actually meant. He was the next Pack Alpha, which meant I would be the next Pack Luna. I swallowed the bitter taste that flooded my mouth and tried to focus on breathing.

The wind picked up, and Zev let out a deep, rumbling growl, sensing something I couldn't see. A twig snapped, and my body jerked. It was so close it made my skin crawl and wolf whimper. I slumped down into the ground, trying to curl into myself.

Zev shifted into his wolf, his shirt ripping at the seams and falling to the ground. The massive black beast before me let out a piercing roar as two other werewolves launched them-selves out of the darkness and onto his back.

Zev's wolf snarled and whipped around, throwing one of them to the ground with a thud. The other rogue embedded its teeth into Zev's shoulder, but he didn't make a sound. Instead, he ran at full speed into the nearest tree, twisted, and slammed the rogue's body hard into the trunk, causing the creature to cry out and release him. Both rogues scurried back onto their feet and circled Zev, trying to edge past him. My guard bared his teeth and growled in warning.

Dara spun around and wrapped her arms tightly around me, pushing me into a tight ball. I squeezed my eyes shut as the Alphas snarled and growled. The sound of heavy bodies and tearing flesh cut into the air around me between guttural roars that hurt my ears. The thick scent of blood hit my nose, and I heaved, unable to control my breathing any longer. Dara's arms tightened, and I started to cry.

The ground shook from heavy paws and quick movements. One of the wolves let out an awful pained sound, then a short yip sliced through the air, followed by a heavy silence.

My heart thundered in my chest, and tears poured down my face as I waited for the fight to erupt again.

After a moment, Dara's arms loosened a bit, but I didn't dare to move. Sitting firmly with my head down and eyes squeezed tightly shut, I listened for any sign of movement.

"My Lady," Dara whispered. "I think—"

Suddenly she was gone, her body completely removed from mine.

I looked up in shock to find Dara struggling in the arms of a massive Alpha I didn't know. His stringy, dark hair hung in his eyes, and blood dripped down his chin and chest.

Zev's wolf-form lay unconscious on the forest floor, blood streaming from a gash on his head. Just to the side of him, another Alpha lay mangled and dead. A massive chunk of flesh was missing from his throat, and blood pooled beneath him.

The wolf holding Dara gripped her hard by the hair and slammed her head into the nearest tree with such force it made the air around me pulse. I choked on a sob as she fell limp to the ground. The rogue smiled wide as he stepped toward me, sweat and dirt covering his naked body.

"Hello, Emmy," he grinned, displaying pointed, bloody teeth.

I kicked my feet out, pushing myself away from him the best I could. My back pressed into the massive rocks, and my breath hitched. I was trapped.

My wolf urged me to run, but I knew it was no use. Even if I could get around the wolf, I could never outrun an Alpha.

"How do you know my name?" I managed to say as I swept my eyes over the area around us, trying to find someone to help or somewhere to hide.

"Come with me, pretty puppy." The words oozed from his mouth.

My eyes flickered just past the scary Alpha and hope-filled my chest. A large, downed tree was illuminated briefly by the parted clouds. It appeared to be hollow. It might have been a trick of the cloud-covered moonlight, but it was something.

Slowly, I stood up. I couldn't help the tears that poured down my face, but I managed to push my head back and look him in the eye. Using all the courage I held in my bones, I forced myself to speak. "Lead the way," I said, thanking the Moon when my voice didn't crack.

The wolf gripped my upper arm, squeezing so tight I could practically feel bruises starting to form. His eyes went wide with excitement as he jerked me hard to his body. I balled up my fists, trying to push him away, but he pulled me closer. His thick scent of musk, dirt, and burning wood filled my lungs and made me gag.

"Let's go," he panted in my ear.

Luck seemed to be on my side, and my heart leapt when he moved toward the fallen tree. I still couldn't tell if it was hollow, but I had no other option. I had to at least try.

I waited until we were just a few steps away, then I jerked myself toward the ground with all my strength. My arm slipped free, and my butt slammed hard into the ground.

The Alpha startled and spun around, but I didn't wait, launching myself forward. I slid as far as I could go into the rotting log. The wood was too soft, and I knew it would only take a few moments for the enraged Alpha to tear it apart and pull me out.

His arm reached in after me, and I kicked as hard as I could, connecting once with his face. The log cracked and shifted, rotting wood and dirt falling into my face and mouth.

The Alpha dug his fingers into the soft tree and pulled himself closer to me, his large body making the log creak and split. His face and teeth were so close. His long fingers wrapped firmly around my ankle, and a wicked grin split his face.

"Got you."

The Woods

Rin

"I AM DONE WITH THIS GAME!" I yelled into the treeline, my fangs lengthening at the promise of blood. "Are you finally ready to fight, or will you keep hiding like cowards?"

My men moved into formation behind me. Their chests rumbled with restrained fury, their wolves restless like mine.

I glanced sideways at my scouts as they dragged the lifeless body of one of my men into the meadow. The rogues had caught them off guard as they trekked the land. It was my mistake to have them venture out, knowing the rogues had been following us, but it was the last one I'd make today. I was done with these fuckers.

The gentle rustle of leaves told me the rogues were edging closer. I wasn't sure how many, but I had twenty of the strongest Alphas Hund Valley had to offer at my back.

This shouldn't take long.

"Come out and die quickly," I mocked. My wolf snarled,

looking forward to the feel of their flesh in his teeth. "If you won't come out, I'll come in." I gave them a moment, not surprised at no sound or movement.

Turning, I nodded to my men. They immediately shifted into their wolves, howling into the night's sky and rushing forward. The hidden rogues moved from their cover and met them halfway.

Wolf clashed into wolf.

Teeth tore into flesh.

Blood already soaked the ground.

I watched as my guards took down several of their lesser trained Alphas and Betas, ending them with little to no fight.

I scanned the meadow to ensure it was empty, and Zev had pulled my mate to safety. Rogues had been known to capture females or Omegas to add to their lawless packs when too many males dominated their numbers. Unfortunately, my Omega had a powerful and distinct scent that lingered long after she left. She wouldn't be that hard to track, and I had been worried something like this might happen since that first night at the camp.

Movement on the other side of the meadow caught my eye, and I readied myself, leaning forward, prepared to shift. A few rogues broke away from their friends and moved through the forest away from the fight.

I could only assume they had caught my mate's scent and were tracking her.

My wolf rushed forward, my muscles flexing and twisting into place, then I charged after them, my heavy paws beating the ground.

Once I broke the treeline, I slowed, moving carefully through the shadows. The bright Moon cut around the clouds, illuminating everything, but the dense forest offered plenty of cover from the light.

Three rogues came into view, and I slipped behind the

trees, staying low to the ground. I enjoyed stalking my prey. The element of surprise always made the fight more fun.

The Alphas raced, clearly chasing something in the wind. One of the wolves with patchy grey fur slowed down and turned, grunting and snarling in my direction. He knew I was here, but he didn't know where—my black pelt working to my advantage in the shadows.

He lowered his body onto the ground and practically crawled toward me, sniffing the air. He was trying to be stealthy, but his clumsy movements thumped and echoed through the otherwise quiet forest.

A twig snapped in the distance, and he cut his eyes sideways. I lunged into the air, pulled his body up by the scruff of his neck, then sank my teeth deep into his flesh. The gush of blood that flooded my mouth filled my body with a burst of adrenaline. The rogue struggled briefly, and I jerked backward, taking his throat with me and ending him quickly.

I immediately set off, following the scent of the other two rogues. I could smell more blood in the distance, and my heart thumped as loudly as my paws on the dense earth.

My mate came into view on the other side of a rocky valley of trees. Her slight body trembled as she stared up at a blood-soaked Alpha in his human form. Fear poured off her, but she held her head high like a true Hund Valley wolf. Zev and Dara lay at her feet, possibly dead, but I didn't have time to dwell on it. Emyanna was my focus.

Tears glistened and dripped down my Omega's cheeks as the Alpha grabbed her arm and pulled her to his sweaty body. I couldn't stop the growl that pushed from my chest, and I picked up my pace.

I moved to launch myself at the bloody Alpha when my mate suddenly dropped to the ground and pushed herself into a fallen tree trunk. Narrowing my eyes, I willed my body faster, relieved I could attack freely without her in the way.

I wrapped my claws around the Alpha's legs as he tried to force himself into the hollow tree. Burying my teeth deep into his thigh, I jerked him back across the rough dirt. His hands emerged, wrapped tightly around Emyanna's ankle, dragging her with him. She screamed and twisted wildly to get out of his hold.

Desperate to remove his disgusting hands from her body, I clamped my jaw around the back of his neck and bit down hard, puncturing his spine and snapping it with ease. His body went limp, hitting the dirt with a thud.

I rose to full height, my chest heaving with heavy breath, and looked into my mate's horrified eyes. I reached for her, but she kicked out, screaming long and loud as tears continued to pour down her face.

Stumbling back, I shifted into my human as fast as my body would allow. Then I grabbed her by the shoulders, shaking her until she finally calmed long enough to look me properly in the face. Relief washed over her soft features, and she closed her eyes, letting out a thankful breath. A loud, long howl cut through the air, and I let her go, scanning the trees.

It wasn't my men, and it was close. Too close.

I spun to grab the Omega, but she was gone. Panic ate at me as I looked around, frantically searching. I found her just off the path kneeling over Dara's unconscious body.

"Come," I ordered, reaching for her arm.

"We have to help them." She jerked away.

"I said come!" Grabbing her again and holding her firmly this time.

"No!" she yelled and struggled as I dragged her away. "Stop! We can't leave them! We have to do something!"

I pulled her to me, gripping her slender arms and looking hard into her big, frightened eyes. She slammed her fists into my chest, a soft grunt pushing from her throat.

"Stop!" I ordered, knowing her Omega wouldn't allow her to disobey me.

Her body immediately softened in my hold, and she moved effortlessly for me as I dragged her further into the woods. Another howl echoed around us, and I stopped to scent the air. They were getting closer.

I picked the Omega up and ran through the trees as fast as I could. She hitched her arms around my neck and dug her nails into my shoulders, holding on tight. The sound of rushing water hit my ears, and I cut a path in its direction.

A narrow river came into view, and I paused, my eyes darting over the area. The dark, rushing waters were illuminated by the waxing Moon. Worry filled me at the possibility of not being able to find somewhere to hide.

Then I saw it.

On the other side of the riverbank, a fallen tree draped itself over a cove of water. It would do. I bolted straight to it and jumped into the freezing river. A field of kunzite crystals gave off a hazy glow through a thick cluster of trees, making the water painfully cold. My mate clawed at my neck, panicking as I moved us through the deep, rough current.

"Hold your breath," I ordered before dunking both of us underwater, navigating my way under the fallen tree trunk and into its mess of branches. Her arms squeezed my neck hard, and I popped back up, breaking the water's surface. She sputtered and coughed, sucking in as much air as she could.

Peeking through the leaves at the water's edge, I checked to make sure no one would be able to see us. I was confident we were hidden well, especially with the water washing away our scents.

Three rogue Alpha's stumbled out of the trees just at the edge of the river, and I tightened my arms around my mate. They appeared to argue briefly before splitting up. One of the

Alphas went back the way she came and the other two moved around the shore, walking straight for us.

Their scents hit my nose as they passed the fallen tree, and fear clawed its way up my throat. I pulled my mate tighter to my chest, hating that she was so close to danger.

My wolf begged me to kill both threats to my Omega immediately, but I stayed put, holding Emyanna's trembling body. She pushed her nose into my neck, and her shoulders shook as if crying, but, to her credit, she made no noise.

THE ALPHAS STAYED near the tree, just off the shore, all fucking night. They argued about their shitty leader, their growing hunger, and their need to find an Omega to release their tension into. My wolf snarled at their words, and my claws lengthened as I held my mate's trembling body. I was growing tired of waiting for them to move the fuck on or for my men to find us and kill them. At this point, I didn't care which.

As dawn approached, my worry bled into fear.

Emyanna had been shaking violently for quite some time now, her distress so thick I could taste it. My wolf bristled at keeping her in such a dangerous situation for so long, and I could only imagine what kind of effect this might have on her. Omegas weren't built for such stress or violence.

I adjusted my hold on my mate, getting another lungful of her thick, sugared scent. My wolf leaned possessively into her, making my hands tighten across her thighs and ass. She was so slight, but the curve of her backside was still impressive, filling my hand nicely.

I couldn't help but squeeze her flesh despite the shit situation.

My muscles ached, and my skin started to go numb. The

cold water smacked into the leaves all around us, kicking up icy droplets into my face and neck. And in all the hours that had passed, Emyanna's hold had yet to soften. She had to be exhausted.

I had just decided to leave her in the water and hope she didn't get pulled away with the current while I fought the two assholes off when the wind picked up. The scent of Hund Valley guards swirled around me, and relief flooded my body.

The two rogues caught the threat in the air as well and disappointed me by running off, not waiting for my men to find them.

I moved my stiff joints and pushed through the wet leaves and rushing water toward the shoreline. The second my feet touched dry ground, I set my mate down as gently as I could.

She jumped back and pushed herself away from me as if filled with an indescribable energy.

"Sir!" a voice called out, and I turned to see one of my sergeants running toward me. "We've been looking for you all night. Are you or your mate injured?"

"We're okay." My voice was strained and tired. "What's the status?" I stepped away from the Omega.

"We took out fifteen of them." My eyes widened at the sheer number of them. It was rare for so many rogues to move together like that. "They got five of us, though," he said, his eyes casting down.

I nodded, my gut twisting at the thought of returning home to mourning families and burial services. My pack fought hard for me, and they didn't deserve to die at the hands of such dishonorable wolves.

I leaned in, speaking quietly so my mate wouldn't hear. "Any of the service staff?" I asked, thinking of her maid. They had grown close rather quickly, and I didn't want her to lose the only friend she had.

"No, Sir," he shook his head. "All the service staff are accounted for. A few injuries, but everyone is okay."

I thanked him and ordered him to circle the area while I escorted Emyanna back to the meadow. I didn't want any surprises between here and there. I was too fucking tired.

Turning, I found my mate staring at the ground, her body trembling uncontrollably. She looked pale and tired, despite the nervous energy radiating off her. I held out a hand to pull her to me, wanting to warm her up, but she jerked away. I didn't blame her hesitation about being touched, especially after what she went through last night. She must be traumatized. But it was dangerous for such a fragile creature to stay soaking wet for such a prolonged period of time. I needed to warm her up.

I reached for her again and, with blazing eyes, she swung her hand through the air and slapped me hard across the face.

The River

Emmy

MY BODY SHOOK WITH RAGE, exhaustion, and disgust. I should have been begging my Alpha for his forgiveness and thanking him for saving my life, but right now, I hated him.

"What the fuck was that for?" Rin yelled, eyes flashing red.

"Don't ever touch me again!" I screamed, shocked when my voice came out strong and sure. "Take me back to the rocks. Take me back to Dara. I need to help her!"

"Dara is fine," he gritted out, stepping toward me. His large body blocked out the rising sun, making me tremble in his shadow, but I stood firm.

"Liar!" I couldn't help it. I was so tired and scared, and all I could think about was him dragging me away from my only friend, forcing me to leave her. "I want to see Dara! I have to see for myself!"

"Shut up and calm the fuck down!" he roared, his patience completely gone.

I was too worked up and worn out to care, but my wolf shivered, begging me to submit to his command. "How can you act like this?" I whispered, enraged by his flippant behavior.

His people were dead, and he had barely reacted, brushing it off like it didn't matter. I wanted to tear him apart. "You made me leave her last night. She risked her life for me, and I abandoned her. How can you not care about that?"

A wet sob bubbled out of my throat as he stood glaring at me. Rin's face darkened with each passing second, and he took a slow, harsh breath. "It's her job to die for you. Stop acting so...so...." He struggled to find the word.

"What?" I snapped, my wolf wailing and trembling at my defiant behavior. "I need to stop acting like what? Like I care about someone? That I have feelings? That I want those I love to be safe?"

"I will not repeat myself. Calm the fuck down!" His pointed teeth flashed as he spoke, and I flinched at the sight.

"You are a monster," I whispered through my tears, balling my fists up. "These are members of your pack. Their deaths should mean something to you. But you act like it doesn't matter."

"You think I don't care? I fucking care!" He closed the small gap between us, his canines lengthening as he spoke. It took everything in me to keep from cowering away. "It fucking kills me that I have to watch my pack die, my friends bleed, their families mourn. But this is the price we have to pay for peace, Omega."

He took a deep, calming breath before continuing, his voice low and dangerous. "There will always be those who want to destroy anyone that lives in peace, and this is what must be done to protect it. The only reason you get to stroll around your gardens and sit in parlors in pretty dresses is because there is someone behind you, fucking protecting you, willing to die for you. You stupid, fucking child!"

My lips trembled, and I struggled to gather what little courage I had left, but I managed to force a few words out in a whisper, "I hate you."

He took a step away from me, rage set in every tense muscle in his massive body. "It's a shame your sister was the Casin daughter to die. Such a waste of good breeding. And now I'm stuck with you."

My body burned with fury, then simmered slow and hot, consuming all my fear. My wolf went silent, then growled low at our mate.

"Sana isn't dead. She ran away." I couldn't help but smirk at the look of shock on his face. "You were taken for a fool because you are one."

For the briefest moment, I thought he was going to hit me. But he didn't. His eyes flashed red as he narrowed them, then he marched off, leaving me by the water.

Swallowing as much of my anger as my body would allow, I forced myself to follow the Alpha back to the meadow, keeping a sizable gap between us.

I wanted to stay put or wander off into the woods to teach him a lesson, but that was just stupid and dangerous. And I needed to get to Dara to apologize for leaving her and make sure she and Zev were okay.

Stopping at the edge of the meadow, I watched Rin stomp toward his men on the other side. A few guards moved around the injured wolves, looking over their wounds and bringing them water. My eyes drifted across the grassy land, and I pressed my lips together to keep from screaming.

The scene before me was horrifying. Bodies littered the ground, ripped up and split open; limbs, guts, and chunks of unidentifiable flesh and fur dotted the land. I turned away from the few faces I recognized as I tried to focus on the group of remaining pack members on the other side.

My feet sunk into the wet, soft earth, and I looked down to see blood pooling up over my skin. Swallowing hard, I pushed my head up and willed myself forward. Mud and blood squished between my toes, and I struggled not to think about the sticky substance coating my feet.

I finally caught sight of Dara, and I couldn't help the whimper that left my lips. I ran to her, sprinting past Rin and flinging myself in her direction. She sat surrounded by a few other injured guards, a look of exhaustion on her beautiful face. Blood streaked her tight, blonde curls, and I could see a sizable cut at the edge of her hairline even from a distance.

"Dara!" I yelled.

She looked up and gasped, relief gripping her features. "My Lady!" She tried to stand, but I rushed her, dropped down, and grabbed her as tightly as I could. She cried and leaned into me, letting me hold her.

After a few blissful moments, she leaned away from me, running her hands over my face and arms. "You aren't hurt?"

I shook my head.

"My Lady, your robes!" she startled, noticing my soaked clothes. "You'll catch a cold. We need to change you and dry your hair."

"We need to clean your wound," I said, looking over the puffy cut. I pulled at the sash tied around my middle and used it to dab away as much of the dried blood as I could. "Dara," I tried to keep my voice steady, "I am so sorry for leaving you last night. Please, forgive me."

"I should be begging you for forgiveness," she said through tears. "I was supposed to protect you, but I didn't. I failed you. Please tell me that rogue...that he didn't, he didn't...take you..." she trailed off, fear quieting her voice.

"He didn't touch me like that," I assured. "Rin found me in time."

"Oh, thank the Moon!" She clutched at her chest. "I was so scared when I woke, and you were gone. I'm so sorry, My Lady. Please forgive me!"

"You have nothing to be sorry for, Dara," I said, hating to see her so upset. After all, I was okay. "You were so brave and wonderful. You were amazing." I pushed my nose into her neck and nuzzled, seeking the comfort of her jasmine-like scent. A deep rumble vibrated the air, and Dara stiffened.

"My Lady," she whispered. She sounded ashamed as she gently pushed at my shoulders. "I'm sorry, but that's too familiar."

I looked up to see Rin on the other side of the guards, glaring at my maid. I returned his awful stare and leaned away from her, not wanting Dara to get in trouble for my behavior. I kept my eyes on the Alpha, trying like hell to convey as much contempt as I could. He wasn't allowed to say he wished me dead then act like a possessive beast mere moments later.

"Don't provoke a wolf," Zev warned, sitting down behind me. "You might not like the consequences."

I spun and let out a very relieved laugh, happy to see my favorite guard safe and smiling. He looked a little rough, a gash above his eye, and his bare chest was scratched up and bruised, but he looked better than some of the other wolves around us.

"I understand new mates can struggle to adjust to each other," he whispered, leaning toward me. "But I would recommend against provoking your Alpha."

My eyes cut back to Rin. He hadn't moved. Still standing firm and glaring, but now at me. My wolf shivered at the look on his face. "I don't know why he cares who I touch. He hates me anyway."

Dara gasped and grabbed my hands. "That's not true!" she practically yelled.

Zev chuckled as if he knew something I didn't. "I can assure you, My Lady. He likes you."

"No," I said firmly, thinking of his words by the river. He wanted nothing to do with me. "He loathes me."

"If that were true, he'd have killed you, not saved you."

"I'm surprised he didn't. He doesn't seem to care who dies."

My eyes drifted to the dead scattered across the meadow. I wondered if any of the wolves who gave their lives had mates or pups waiting for them back home.

"I don't want to overstep, My Lady," Zev said in a kind tone. "But I can assure you, Rin cares very much for you and his people. He might not show his grief, but it's an Alpha's job to hold his people together, not fall apart with them."

I looked up at Zev then Dara. Both smiled politely, neither scolding me even though they probably should have. Shame hit me hard, and I twisted my fingers, feeling stupid.

"I'm sorry," I whispered, tears starting to fall, embarrassed by what I said.

Wiping at my cheeks, I sniffled hard. I was so sick of crying. I would rip out my eyes if it meant I'd never shed another tear out of weakness ever again.

"Don't be sad, My Lady." Dara gave me a soft smile, holding my hands. "These wolves died doing their job. The job of a warrior. They will be honored and loved for their sacrifice."

"Will we take them with us?" I asked, my eyes flickering to the remains.

"No," Zev said simply. "They'll stay here and feed the ground they fell on."

"What are their families going to do?" I asked carefully, not wanting to offend them. "What are their friends supposed to do?" I whispered, glancing at the guards around us.

"Their families will honor and mourn them. And the rest

of us will wait for the next fight." He gave me a soft smile. And while I hated his answer, I appreciated how he said it. He was very kind.

"The guards should probably eat," I said, feeling useless and fidgety.

"We're not hunting this morning," Zev said. "We'll patch ourselves up, then move on. Hunting takes too much time, and Rin is anxious to leave this land."

I scanned the meadow, looking for the large cart that held most of our supplies. It sat near the treeline, overturned and stuck in the mud. The horses were gone, the ties cut, and all its contents were scattered across the ground. But a familiar basket caught my eye, sitting upright, its lid still firmly in place.

I moved toward it, swiping a cup off the ground and blowing in it to clean out some flecks of dirt and grass. Popping off the lid, my stomach growled at the delicious mixture of nuts and seeds. Plunging the cup inside, I pulled out a massive helping. I wanted to pour the whole thing into my mouth, but I held back and turned to the guards behind me. I needed to make sure they were fed first. They had sacrificed so much more than I had, and it was the only way I could think to thank them.

The Meadow

Rin

MY WOLF HAD NEVER BEEN SO conflicted before. He was enraged that I would speak to our mate in such a harsh manner but also consumed with the urge to race back to Casin and slaughter every single member of Hector's pack for forcing her on me.

Emyanna was not the mate promised, nor was she the obedient Omega her father had assured. I was not in the habit of tolerating those that tested my authority or attempted to play with my honor, and, one way or another, Hector would pay for this.

Inhaling a long, calming breath, I readied myself to reprimand my mate. She needed instruction on how she was allowed to speak and conduct herself around me. The Omega was lucky all I gave her was a few angry words and not a well-deserved smack to her ass for her defiance.

I took a few steps toward Emyanna just as she jumped up, rushing toward our overturned supplies. She scurried around the guards, pouring rabbit feed into their hands. Alphas didn't eat scavenger food, but they smiled and bowed their heads anyway, thanking her profusely.

She was trying to be nice. I understood that. But it was still stupid.

My mate rushed past me to refill her cup, and I leaned into her scent. I groaned, hating how much my wolf had come to like her. It had to be the mating bite. It pulls two wolves together, fusing them with a deep, primal connection. And it was fucking with my head.

I should be mated to Sana. A strong female with a decent education and understanding of how the world worked. Not this frightened pup, with no grasp on reality.

Emyanna seemed to not understand that our union ensured Hund Valley's future. Whether she liked it or not, our lives were deemed more important than those in our service.

Saving her was my priority and always would be, even though it killed me to walk away from Zev's unconscious body. He was like blood to me, and I left him for her safety. She should respect that, not condemn me for it.

I turned and was taken aback to see my mate standing directly in front of me. She was looking up into my face and not at her feet for once. Her deep brown eyes flared, and she held up the cup filled with nuts and seeds, waiting.

Slowly, I brought my hand up and cupped it, assuming that's what she wanted. Keeping those wide eyes on me, she tipped the cup and sloppily poured its contents into my hand, half of it falling to the ground. Then she turned without a word and stalked off.

"I don't want to speak out of turn, Sir," Zev said, stepping up next to me. "But you might want to think about making this work. Forever is a very long time to be bound to someone, and it might be more pleasant if you at least liked each other a little."

"The next time you don't want to speak out of turn, don't," I said. He was right but fuck him for saying it. "I have much more important things to deal with right now than making sure my mate is skipping with joy at her current circumstances."

"Of course, Sir." Zev bowed his head, all amusement gone. "We're ready to leave as soon as you give the command."

I nodded and dismissed him, cutting Emmy one more glance before turning my attention back to my men.

After tending to everyone's wounds and grabbing what supplies we could carry—our cart and carriage now useless without horses—we pushed on. The group traveled at a steady pace and without complaint, covering a lot of ground in a short amount of time.

I was worried about forcing the few Betas in our company and my mate to go so far without a proper break, but none of them protested. We were probably only a day or two from home, and I was desperate to get there. I wasn't sure the remaining rogues were done with us, and the fact that we took down so many of them made me wonder how many more they had at their base camp.

We kept moving as night settled, and the stars glimmered brightly. I had hoped we'd see the edge of Lake Vita before being forced to stop for the night, but I was starting to think we weren't as close as I had initially thought. Defeated, I decided to make camp.

"Sir," Zev pulled my attention as my guards set up around my mate and her maid. "I think it would be wise for you to sleep in the center of the guards with Lady Emmy tonight."

"No." I kept my eyes on the dark forest around us, not in the mood to be anywhere near the obnoxious Omega.

"Sir," he said with a tone that told me he wasn't going to

let it go. "We thought we lost both of you last night. Hours of frantic searching have left the men on edge. It would be kind to them to have both of you in a safe and central location. I think we'll all sleep better knowing exactly where you are."

I popped my neck and scanned the trees around me once more before cutting my eyes to my mate. She snuggled into her maid, their arms circled around one another. My wolf bristled, not liking someone touching what was mine and covering my Omega in their scent. I stiffened and pushed down a growl before giving Zev a curt nod. My wolf's chest swelled, and I scowled, not in the mood for his shit either.

Walking through the guards, I stopped to check on injuries and made sure everyone was drinking their rations. A few asked if I would be on patrol tonight, and they visibly relaxed when I informed them I'd be sleeping near my mate. Fucking Zev. Always has to be right.

Once she was asleep, I took my place next to Emyanna, moving slowly not to wake her. I was thankful not to have to suffer her glare.

Tucking an arm behind my head, I closed my eyes. But my peace didn't last long as the Omega rolled into me, flinging a leg over my groin.

My wolf scented her long and deep, making my chest rumble and cock swell. My bulge pressed right up against the inside of her soft thigh, and my fangs punched out painfully fast.

Trying to adjust my now raging erection, I shifted my hips only to bite back a swear. The heat from her body rubbed my shaft just right, and I froze, all too aware of my surroundings.

My men were all around us, in the middle of the rogue-infested woods, and the Omega was still under-fucking-age.

Rage boiled within me, and my claws pushed against my fingertips, making my hands ache.

Ignoring every basic instinct pulsing through my body, I stared up at the Moon, cursing her for tying me to something so disrespectful and young.

Hund Valley

Emmy

THE RAIN in the spring was by far my favorite of all the seasons. It was the rebirth of the flowers and a promise of nature returning home. I was so pleased when I woke to that wonderful scent filling my nose, and I smiled before even opening my eyes.

I pushed myself into Dara's side, loving how the wind wrapped me in that beautiful aroma. Moving my hands up and over her, I froze when I realized the firm, large wolf next to me wasn't my maid.

I jerked back and snapped my eyes open to see Rin's dark eyes looking down at me, his expression hard and tight. Why did he always look so angry?

"We're leaving in ten minutes," he said in a deep, flat tone before getting up and walking off.

My wolf let out a soft whine.

Because of the mating bite, my wolf's tie to the Alpha was so much stronger than my tie to Rin. And my wolf was devastated that the only time he had really spoken to me was to tell me how disappointed he was that I wasn't Sana.

I just wished he would offer me a kind word or soft look. Not that I deserved it. I was a pretty horrible mate so far too.

Brushing my fingers over my mating bite, I couldn't help but feel a little lost. It was weird being bound to someone that didn't like you. It was confusing and scary, and, right now, I just wanted to go home.

Dara smiled as she handed me a bit of breakfast, and I struggled to return the friendly gesture, my wolf too sad.

We ate quickly then set off on our original trail.

The guards seemed to be in a better mood, most of them already on the mend. Dara and I cursed an Alpha's ability to heal so much faster than us lower-statused wolves. However, Dara's cut did look much better already, the swelling almost completely gone.

Just before midday, a stir of howling and cheering cut through the air. The scouts had spied the lake that bordered Hund Valley, causing everyone to pick up their pace. Rin smiled when he heard the news, and I was shocked. I had yet to see the Alpha give a proper smile. It flowed through his body, crinkling his eyes, and I couldn't help but smile too.

Rin ordered a pair of guards to shift and take the lead, running ahead to inform the village of our arrival. Dara said it would still be a few hours until we reached the gates, but the thought of sleeping in a real bed gave my feet renewed purpose.

The heat of the day was starting to burn off when I caught sight of Hund Valley's border wall. I gasped at its size. The village was easily three times the size of Casin, if not bigger.

The guards talked excitedly, their usually stiff demeanor falling away as we got closer to their home. A few Alphas ran up ahead as villagers rushed out of the gates to greet them. So many wolves of every status crowded at the entrance, pouring out to greet us. Everyone was smiling and cheering, and pups stood on their toes to get a better view.

Rin stopped directly in front of me, blocking my path. I looked up at him confused, but Dara moved next to me, understanding what the Alpha wanted. She worked quickly, smoothing down my hair and the front of my robes. I suddenly realized that I hadn't had a proper bath or changed my clothes in days. I was sure I looked brutal, but there was no helping it. At least my new home would greet me as I was, a mess.

Once satisfied, Dara turned to Rin. "Ready, Sir."

Rin faced the village gates and grabbed my hand. I jerked back, not meaning to, but his touch only reminded me of just how upset I was. I needed to get past his words by the river, but it hurt.

It hurt more than I was willing to admit.

It was just easier to be mad.

Taking a quick step back, I prepared for the Alpha to yell, but he didn't say a word. His massive form loomed over me, his anger pulsing in the air and burning through our bond.

"Go," he said to Dara, not bothering to look at her, and she rushed off.

My wolf shivered, and it took everything in me to keep my body from doing the same. I squeezed my hands together, trying to push the Alpha's agitation away. I didn't want it to consume me and force me into a panic. Not right before walking through my new home with so many eyes on me.

"Omega," he growled in warning.

I hated that he never called me by my name. Mates called

each other by their names because it was intimate and loving, but he didn't want either of those things with me. I was just another Omega to him.

"The pack is excited to meet their next Luna, and since several of Hund Valley's guards have died to bring you here safely, the very least you can do for your new pack is to look happy with your mate."

His narrowed eyes bore into mine until I finally held out my hand. I didn't want to touch him, scared he'd be able to feel how tender my heart was, but he was right. I needed to be gracious for my new pack.

Rin ignored my outstretched hand and placed a forced smile on his face. I stared up at him, my arm still extended, feeling stupid. Why wasn't he moving?

He raised his eyebrows and widened his grin pointedly. Finally understanding, I pulled the corners of my lips up into, what I hoped, was a convincing smile. He nodded and took my hand, pulling me forward.

My wolf preened the second the Alpha's large hand closed around mine. A slight shiver ran up my spine from deep within me, and I closed my eyes, trying to ignore it.

The desire my body and wolf held for the Alpha next to me only made me feel worse.

This was nothing like my storybook romances. So far, it just hurt.

I sighed, quieting my thoughts and focusing on the massive village in front of me.

The crowd swelled and bustled as we approached the gates. So many wolves lined the beautifully paved streets. It was shocking to see so many happy faces. They bowed and yelled out blessings for healthy pups and a prosperous reign, Omegas waved colorful scarves in the air toward us, and pups tossed bundles of lavender and lilies at our feet.

I squeezed Rin's hand, praying my shaking knees wouldn't give out, and he was kind enough to squeeze mine back.

Hund Valley was just so big. It dwarfed Casin a hundred times over. My old pack was a simple village at the foot of the mountains with little log cabins and vast gardens. This was a city. And it seemed that every wolf that lived here had poured out into the streets to stare at me.

By the time we made it to the packhouse, which more closely resembled a grand manor from one of my many books back home, I finally understood my parents' fear. Hund Valley could destroy Casin without even trying. They needed this alliance to ensure their survival.

Casin was small and vulnerable. Hund Valley was big and powerful.

It should have made me happy, but it scared me even more. I would eventually be their Luna, and this would be a *lot* of responsibility.

The inside of the packhouse was just as intimidating. Tall ceilings, ornate fixtures, and unnerving paintings of old, angry Alphas covered the walls. I was scared to touch anything, the delicate pieces of furniture looking more like art than for actual living.

"Rinnie!" A bright and bubbly Omega, not too much younger than me, rushed toward us and flung his arms around Rin. The Alpha smiled and lifted him off his feet, squeezing him around the middle. The young Omega had the same tan skin and dark hair as Rin, but his curls were more vibrant and wild.

"Have you been good?" Rin asked, setting the Omega back down.

"Always," he smiled, his hands tucked behind his back and a look of mischief in his big, dark eyes. "Stop being a meanie and introduce me to my new sister," he said, playfully twisting his lithe hips.

"Quin. This is my mate, Lady Emyanna," Rin motioned to me. "Emyanna. My brother, Omega Quin."

"It's a pleasure to meet you." I bowed, wanting to be polite and set a good impression, but he caught me by the arms and pulled me into the warmest hug. Quin stood a few inches taller than me, but I still wanted to put him in my pocket and treasure him forever. He was just so sweet.

"Let's not be formal," he giggled. "It's boring and silly. But more importantly, you have to tell me all about your trip and every stupid thing my brother did."

I loved him instantly.

He radiated the most beautiful energy, and I wanted to bathe in it.

"Will you show Lady Emyanna to my room?" Rin asked his brother, his face pulling back to his usual serious frown. "I need to speak with Father."

"Of course," Quin chirped, grabbing my hand.

He ushered me toward a large, winding staircase with a thick, white railing but slowed when Zev passed. The Alpha bowed his head silently at the Omega next to me, and I couldn't help but notice the blush that crept over Quin's cheeks. It was adorable.

The packhouse was so clean and elegant. The tall, white walls brought all the focus to the large windows that spanned the length of the halls. Outside them sat the most beautiful garden I had ever seen. It was filled with lilies of all shades, tall spruce trees, and a cluster of willows that swayed over the most inviting pond I had ever seen.

"I am so happy to have another Omega in the packhouse," Quin sighed as we walked down a long corridor. "There's way too much Alpha under this roof."

"I know how you feel," I sighed. "I was the first Omega born in my family in six generations. I broke my family's true Alpha status."

"True Alphas? Wow." Quin raised his eyebrows. "Is your whole village like that?"

"For the most part. Mostly Alphas and a few Betas, not many Omegas at all. And those that do live there aren't really allowed to leave their homes." His eyes widened, his mouth slightly ajar, and I suddenly regretted bringing it up.

A pang gripped my heart, and my eyes welled up. I didn't want to cry. I didn't miss my village, so there was no reason to be upset, but tears fell down my cheeks anyway. I was just so overwhelmed. Everything had changed so quickly, and talking about my old pack only made me realize I was never going home.

"Oh, Emyanna!" Quin whispered, letting out a sad sigh and wrapping his arms around me. "Please don't cry, my sweet sister. You'll make me cry, and then we'll both need a bath."

I laughed. He was just so light and cozy.

"Emmy," I whispered. "Please, call me Emmy."

"Emmy," he smiled, squeezing my hands and pulling me down the hallway again. "I bet you miss home real bad."

I nodded. It seemed a much simpler answer.

"We don't have to talk about it if you don't want to," he whispered, his voice suddenly low and reassuring, "but I'm here if you need to." It was as if someone had sucked all the bubbles out of his personality but left the sweetness. "Are you excited for tonight?"

"What's tonight?" I asked, thankful for the change in subject.

"The final ritual for your bonding."

I stopped in my tracks. "Are you kidding me? How many things does your pack make you do just to be mated?" I knew I was whining, but I didn't care. I was too tired.

"We like to drag things out," Quin laughed. "But don't worry. It's just a blessing from our temple priest." He leaned in, whispering as if scandalized, "She blesses your marital bed."

It hit me hard. I was a mated Omega.

My mouth went dry as I thought of my actual purpose here. To provide pups for my Alpha. I meant what I said to Rin at the river, I never wanted him to touch me again, but I knew that wasn't possible. I couldn't refuse him. I'd be cast out or maybe even killed for being a horrible mate and useless Luna. Rin might even attack Casin for my treason.

I took a deep breath and accepted my fate. While all I ever wanted in life was a mate to love and adore me, I'd do what I had to and settle for what I was given. This was my purpose here. I didn't have any other choice.

"And here is your bedroom!" Quin practically sang as he held out his hands, waving them in front of a set of large, white double doors.

He pushed one heavy door open to reveal a spacious room with a balcony overlooking the gardens. The space was surprisingly simple, not much furniture other than a cluttered desk, one stiff-looking chair, and a very intimidating bed in the center. I looked all around, but my eyes kept pulling back to that damn bed and what I would eventually have to do on it.

Quin babbled about the things he wanted to do together, but my mind pulled to memories of the bonding ceremony, then the night that followed.

Rin was so mean, not bothering to hide his disappointment at being stuck with me. The thought of laying with him now was just as scary as that first night at the camp.

I tensed, remembering how he snapped at me for every little thing, ordering me around, rejecting me, then cleaning my mark.

I grazed my fingertips over my throat.

Rin cleaning my mark...

His lips were so soft, and his chest was so warm and firm pressed against me. My mind swirled with memories of the way he smelled and the feel of his large hands moving over my back, holding me so safe and tight.

My wolf leaned into the memories, her adoration for our strong Alpha swirling hard within me.

Something deep inside me twisted, and I pressed my knees together, suddenly nervous and excited and confused all at once.

The Packhouse

Rin

I LEFT my mate with Quin and headed toward my father's study. He sat in his favorite chair behind a cluttered desk, a book in one hand and a glass of barley whiskey in the other. This was how he spent most of his days since my mother's passing, leaving me to take on all of the responsibilities even though I wasn't the Pack Alpha yet.

It broke my heart to see him like this, but it enraged me more. He loved our mother dearly, but she'd been gone a little over a year, and life had to go on. He still had two sons to care for, one underage, and a pack to lead. But it was as if the old wolf simply decided nothing was worth doing now that she was gone.

So he drank and picked fights, and it pissed me the fuck off.

Only sloppy Alphas gave away their self-control so easily.

If I were a better son, I'd still try to carry him through his grief, but my sympathy dried up long ago. It was hard to respect a wolf intent on abandoning his pack responsibilities.

"Rin!" my father yelled once he noticed me, fumbling to put down his book. He had obviously been indulging in his drink for quite some time now.

I gave him my report, letting him know of the rogues and our lost guards. I was eager to get this over with, so I could bathe and finally sleep. My body was so worn, and I hadn't been able to move without tension in my neck since the bonding ceremony.

My father nodded and waved off his stewards so they could plan fitting services for the dead. Our village would hold a festival in their honor and praise them for giving their lives to protect our pack and its future.

"Tell me, my son," my father said once we were alone. "How is everything with that Omega of yours?"

"Fine."

"Was she as sweet as she looked?" He raised his eyebrows, and my wolf snarled at his implication.

Keeping my expression blank, I stared and refused to answer. Seeming to understand my anger, he sucked in a deep breath and stood up, fixing his face to hold a more appropriate expression.

"I want you to know that I approve of how you've handled this. You've taken responsibility for the situation and assured our alliance with Casin by mating that Omega. And while I know her age was an issue for you, I'm glad you overlooked it in the name of duty. I just hope we can count on an heir soon."

"Of course, Father."

"I cannot stress how important an heir is, Rin," he said in a deep, weighty tone. He looked at me from under his heavy lids, an expression he saved for when he was prepared to lash out to make his point. "Quin too easily believes in love and other such ridiculous daydreams. I can't trust him to find a proper Alpha that would be worthy of leading this pack. It's all on you to secure our future."

I nodded, knowing better than to say anything he might perceive as a challenge.

"But seriously, son. Don't beat yourself up for it too much." His voice was suddenly loud and animated again.

He walked around the desk and smacked my shoulder, his movements wide and exaggerated. "A few weeks away from her coming of age isn't something to dwell on. Hell, even a few years wouldn't have been that much of an issue. After all, Omegas were created to satisfy Alphas."

I went stiff at his words, the muscle in my jaw ticking. *A few years?*

A coming of age was not something to be taken lightly. Anyone willing to corrupt an innocent pup before the Moon approved of their maturity wasn't worthy to walk among civilized wolves.

I pushed my eyes to the floor, unable to look my father in the eye. I didn't understand how he could have such an easy opinion, especially since his youngest pup and mate were both Omegas. My wolf snarled at the thought of anyone touching Quin before his twentieth year, my temper flaring dangerously close to the surface.

I turned to leave, not waiting for my father to excuse me. It was rude, but I was too angry.

"Rin!" he yelled before I could reach the door. "I received a letter from Hector." He held up a piece of parchment with a broken seal on it. "He wants to formally thank you for taking the Omega after her sister's untimely death. He plans to leave Casin soon and should be here at the start of the next full Moon. Let your mate know."

I nodded and left.

While I didn't know much about Emyanna's relationship with her family, I could plainly see it wasn't on the best of terms. Especially considering how easily they lied about one daughter dying while seeming to not care about the other leaving. Not a single one of them even tried to bid her farewell.

Grabbing the railing on the staircase, I placed a foot on the bottom step before stopping. My mind flooded with images of my mate's mother glaring at her as she laid on the temple floor crying, the frightened look in Emyanna's eyes as she trembled next to me covered in blue paint at the camp, and her slight body pressed against mine in the cold river. She had spent almost every moment of the last few weeks in fear. And I suddenly felt guilty for being so harsh with her.

Closing my eyes, I imagined my Omega's sweet scent surrounding me. My wolf pushed closer to the surface, wanting to be near her, to claim her. But she was still a pup, and I was suddenly nervous about finding her in my bed.

I was exhausted and on edge, and my self-control was razor thin.

Turning around, I immediately rushed through the pack-house toward the gardens. I stepped outside and set off at a quick pace, shifting into my wolf the second I hit the edge of the property. Then I ran.

I ran fast, and hard, and long. The air in my lungs pinched my chest, and my muscles ached. I raced through the trees and around the rocks, not stopping until I hit the border wall, sprinting straight for it and hitting it with my back.

I wanted to think of anything other than Emyanna's fierce brown eyes and sweet, sugar scent. I hated that she wedged herself into my mind, burrowing under my skin and destroying my willpower. I just needed a few moments without her consuming my every thought, but her face followed me even out here.

Falling onto the ground, I sucked in as much air as my lungs would allow. My mind swirled with the feel of Emmy's soft skin and the curve of her sweet body sleeping next to me. I burned with frustration and rage, and lust. And my wolf let out a vicious, painful roar, reveling in it.

AFTER STOPPING to wash in the pond, I made my way up the stairs to my room. Opening the door, I found my mate sitting in the center of my bed in a pale blue nightdress and a book about strategic battle in her hands.

"Are you interested in waging war?" I asked, raising an eyebrow.

She slowly closed the book, flinging it onto the bed next to her. "It was either this, or poetic words of warriors passed." She sighed. "You don't have many options in here."

"If you like to read, we have a library."

Her face lit up, and she clapped her hands together, but just as quickly, her expression fell, and she cleared her throat. "I would love to see it," she said a little formally.

"It's not as big as the one in Vaesen, but it's decent in size."

"Right now, I'd settle for a temple pamphlet on prayer and charity," she mumbled.

I glanced around the room, noticing pillar candles set along the floor and around the bed. I had forgotten about the ritual blessing.

"Omega," I said, feeling the need to warn her about my father's expectations. He was sure to make some kind of inappropriate comment the second he saw her, and I wanted her prepared. "The Pack Alpha will be expecting an heir soon. With your coming of age fast approaching, I wanted to remind you of your purpose here."

She stiffened and crossed her arms over her chest. "I know what I'm here for," she said softly. "You don't have to tell me like it's a threat."

My wolf snarled and tensed at the look on her face. She might have sounded meek, but her eyes were pure fire.

"Just to be clear, you will *not* talk to me like this in front of anyone. Ever." I was so exhausted. My body hurt, and my mind was a fucking mess. "The fact that you would dare to challenge me like this in any situation is completely unacceptable, and right now, I don't have the fucking energy or patience for your shit."

A shiver worked through her body, and she bared her throat involuntarily but quickly recovered. Those big eyes of hers were just as hard, and her jaw clenched with barely controlled rage. She might have physically submitted to me, but just barely.

And it set me off.

"Omega," I growled deep and low, prepared to remind her who the dominant one was in this room.

"Emmy!" she snapped, her cheeks growing pink as her anger spilled over. "My name is Emmy. Not Omega. I am not a stranger or pup for you to scold. I am your mate and will one day be your Luna."

Her eyes were wild with fear and anger, and her lips trembled, but she held firm in her glare. Not a tear in sight.

It was about fucking time. I was sick of watching her cry.

"You want to be my mate? My Luna?" My hands itched to slap her ass red. "You want to take on the responsibilities of this pack and provide an heir? Is that what you want?" My blood burned as hot as the look in her eyes. "I should just end this game and fucking take you now. Put a pup in you and shut you up. Then I'd never have to bother with you again. Both our duties fulfilled and done!"

A slip of distress pushed from her throat, but she didn't

move to submit this time, staying completely still. I stepped closer to the bed, forcing my dominance out into the room.

She let out a shuddering breath, and her chin tipped up slightly, then she stopped. Her whole body shook as she held firm, eyes filled with silent defiance.

My wolf roared within me as I waited for her to yield to her Alpha. He wanted me to fuck her into submission and fix her fucking attitude once and for all.

Emmy's lips twitched, flashing the briefest glimpse of her teeth, and I was on her before she could blink. I pinned her hands over her head, struggling to cling to what little control I had left.

"Do I need to forcefully put you in your place?" I snarled, squeezing her wrists as my eyes pulsed red with lust and fury. The urge to take her was so fucking intense.

Her eyes went wide with shock before she set her face, holding her mouth in a tight pout. I was sure she was trying to look fierce, but it was just cute. I fucking hated it.

I buried my face in her neck, dragged my teeth over her collarbone, up the juncture of her shoulder, all the way up to my mating bite. Piercing her flesh with the tips of my fangs, I hoped the pain would remind her who her Alpha was and settle her wolf. But it had the opposite effect on me.

Her sweet scent hit my tongue as I sucked at her skin, making my cock plump and wolf restless with desire. Inhaling deeply, I closed my eyes, and my mouth watered. All my rage melted into pure, helpless lust.

Emmy arched her back up into me as I hovered over her. I didn't know if she was trying to free herself or pull me closer, but it made my body flash hot and wolf thrill.

Pushing my tongue out, I moved up the expanse of her throat, tasting her sweet skin. The softest breath left her lips, and my cock twitched. Forcing myself to lean up and look at her, I searched for the fear in her eyes, hoping it would bring me back to my senses. But I was shocked to see her looking up at me with the darkest expression, her eyes hooded with just as much desire.

She laid quietly beneath me, her hands over her head and her legs slightly parted. She looked so submissive and willing, her eyes practically drawing me into her soft form.

She licked her pink lips, drawing my eyes to them. Slowly, I leaned down, prepared to claim her mouth, then her body. She softened in my hold and tilted her chin up, inviting me closer.

Ghosting my lips over hers, I was so fucking ready to fall into her sweet scent and claim what was mine.

A quick knock on the door made me jerk as my father burst into the room.

"Slow down there, son." His voice filled the otherwise quiet room.

I pushed up and away from my mate as fast as I could. Emmy curled into a ball as he moved closer to the bed, tucking her legs up into her nightdress and hugging them tightly.

"I know you must be eager," he hooked his thumbs in his belt, "but I'm sure you can wait a few minutes for the blessing."

The temple priest entered the room and bowed, followed by the family healer. I tilted my head slightly, confused as to his presence. My father followed my eyes to the healer and cleared his throat.

"I've asked Beta Sami to look over your Omega. I want to make sure she's in good health and find out if we need to be planning a celebration of pups anytime soon."

Emmy straightened her back and snapped her head to me, her mouth slightly open in shock. I knew she was thinking the same as me. Would he be able to tell we hadn't properly coupled yet?

"Father," I said as politely as I could. "It's far too early to check for pups, isn't it?"

Beta Sami shifted his blue eyes uncomfortably at my determined father before forcing a smile and speaking carefully. "It is. But the Pack Alpha insisted. And checking an Omega over after such a long journey is never a bad idea."

Emmy let out a dramatic sob and threw her hands over her face. "Don't make me, Alpha!" she begged me through her fingers. "It's bad luck. The Moon will punish our young!" Tears dripped down her cheeks as she cradled her flat stomach. "It brings bad luck to touch an Omega before the signs of carrying young start. Please, Alpha. Don't hurt our pup!" She sobbed harder.

I had to give her credit. She was much better at this than her mother. The old woman's excessively fake crying back at the Casin temple was exceptionally shoddy. Hector bought it, but I could easily see through her game. Emmy, on the other hand...

This looked real, but I knew her tears too well by now.

"Father," I said. "It goes against her beliefs. In the Casin pack, newly mated wolves aren't touched by anyone other than their mate." I gave him an apologetic smile, knowing he'd back off. He was hopeless at handling emotional Omegas. It was why Quin got away with so much.

"Please calm down, My Lady," Sami whispered in an understanding tone. "I won't touch you. Just promise me, you'll let me know if you feel sick or bad in any way?"

Emmy nodded and calmed a bit, wiping at her cheeks with the back of her hand. I reached out and squeezed her shoulder, trying to play the part of the loving mate. She leaned into my touch and gave me a beautiful smile that clutched my chest and stole my ability to think straight.

I settled next to my mate on the edge of the bed, in a daze.

I was eager for the ritual to be over and done. I needed

everyone gone so I could get some sleep and hopefully shake the overwhelming pull I felt to the Omega next to me. I wasn't weak and was more than capable of resisting her, but I was too exhausted at the moment to fight my wolf and my desires.

Keeping my eyes on the priest, I tried to focus on her words and not the honey scent that still lingered on my tongue.

Breakfast

Emmy

"Good morning, My Lady," Dara hummed as she opened the curtains.

I stretched out and immediately looked for Rin. The quilt on his side of the bed was smoothed over, and his pillow was cool to the touch. I couldn't ignore that I was a little upset he wasn't here.

After the priest finished her prayers, we went to bed, not speaking a word about what had happened before his father barged into the room.

I laid awake for hours, obsessing about every moment—the mean things Rin said, how his eyes flashed red as I defied him, the feel of his large hands wrapped so perfectly around my wrists and the brief moment when I thought he was going to kiss me.

Oh, how I wanted him to kiss me.

His warm touch made me feel so safe and calm. Even if he didn't really want me, I could pretend when he held me.

My wolf yearned for his touch, and if I closed my eyes and ignored the Alpha's anger, I could pretend he yearned for mine.

"Alpha Rin requested I order you some new clothes," Dara said, pulling me from my thoughts. "They should be here within the week, but you can wear the clothes you brought from your old pack until then."

She moved to a large chest that I recognized as Sana's. It made sense that her luggage was here. I just wished I had been able to collect a few of my own things before being ushered to the temple.

"Your new robes will be in the Hund Valley colors," Dara continued. "You look so lovely in blue." She motioned to my nightdress.

Smiling, I looked down at her compliment. I wasn't used to someone being so nice to me, and it was a little awkward. I wasn't sure what to say.

Dara opened the chest and pulled out a lavender and green dress, setting it on the bed. I ran my hands over the familiar fabric, remembering the last time I saw it.

Sana wore it just a few days before the bonding ceremony. It caused an argument between her and my father when he insisted she change. He hated how short it was and how her breasts nearly leapt out of the top. When she refused, purposely popping a few buttons and pushing her cleavage out, he fell into a rage and ripped the dress right off her. I spent that afternoon crying alone in the garden.

I missed her so much.

Sucking in a harsh breath, I pushed myself out of bed, determined not to cry. There was no sense dwelling over my life in Casin anymore. That Emmy was gone.

I was thankful to find the dress didn't have the same

effect on my figure as Sana's—I wouldn't have been able to pull it off. The soft material was loose on top and, with how much shorter I was than my sister, it hit my knees comfortably. It was a little snug around my waist, but it looked okay.

"Lavender compliments you, My Lady," Dara smiled.

"If I asked you to call me Emmy, would you?" I asked, nervous it might be inappropriate. She was a staff member, and such a request was very personal, but Dara was the closest thing I had to a friend. And it would be so nice if we could treat each other as such.

She hesitated, glancing around as if being watched.

"What about when we're alone?" I asked, hopeful.

She thought for a moment before finally smiling. "Okay," she whispered, "Emmy." She covered her bright smile with her hands and giggled as if she had done something naughty. I couldn't help but laugh with her.

Dara grabbed my brush and set to work, smoothing out my tangles.

"Alpha Rin has also asked me to arrange an instructor to come in to provide lessons on conduct and etiquette. Would you like anything else?"

"What do you mean?" I turned to look at her over my shoulder.

"Anything else you'd like to learn? Painting, writing, poetry, pottery? Whatever interests you, My Lady."

I gave her a teasing glare.

"Emmy." She pressed her lips together.

"I don't know." I shook my head. "What should a Luna know?"

"This isn't for being a Luna. It's just something for you to enjoy."

Moving my eyes to my lap, I tried to figure out what I might like to do, but I had no idea. In my old pack, I spent most of my time hiding in the library. No one ever bothered me to do anything outside of staying out of the way.

"You don't have to decide now." Dara smoothed the brush through my hair, pulling all the tension from my shoulders.

I nodded, a little light of excitement growing in my chest. While I might never have the adoring mate I had always dreamed of, I could have a life here laced with a little fun and something new. The thought made me smile wide.

Dara escorted me down the stairs and through the winding hallways, to the family dining room. It was a massive space with a large table that could easily fit twenty Alphas. The walls were the same white as the rest of the house, with a lovely painting of a field of lilies and another one of a very creepy Alpha with a dark scowl and wild hair.

"It's like he hates watching people eat," Quin snorted just behind me. I spun around to greet him, and he squeezed me with a fierce energy. "Did you sleep well?"

"I did, thank you," I said, happy not to sit alone.

Quin led me to the chair next to his and chatted away about all the amazing things he wanted to show me around the packhouse and village. I leaned into the bubbly Omega's words as Rin and the Pack Alpha walked in, both looking very serious.

Rin's eyes moved over my face, and he seemed lost, just looking at me, before finally clearing his throat and taking a seat across from me. He nodded as his father continued to speak, but his eyes kept pulling back to my face. I was sure he was looking forward to yelling at me once he had the chance. There was no way he would let me get away with how I acted last night.

Once Alpha Rollen settled, breakfast was served. I wasn't used to such formality. I usually ate in the kitchens unless my father ordered otherwise. It was the only chance I had to talk with wolves other than my family, and the kitchen staff were always very polite about my presence, letting me crack the eggs and stoke the stone fire.

This was very intimidating in comparison.

I had never seen so many forks for one meal, and I wasn't sure where to start. This was probably a part of the education everyone was so upset I hadn't received.

"Emyanna," Rin said a little too loudly. He looked stiff and a little...*nervous?*

I smiled and looked up at him expectantly, trying to play the part of the happy mate.

"How..." he cleared his throat, "how did you sleep?"

"Very well, thank you." I smiled. He seemed off. "And you?"

"Very well...as well." Rin let out a pained sigh and gave his head a quick jerk at his words. Quin did a poor job of stifling a giggle and raised his eyebrows at me in a suggestive manner. I had no idea what he was trying to say.

"Are you okay, my boy?" the Pack Alpha asked, patting Rin's shoulder.

"Yes," Rin groaned. He looked up at me, then noticed Quin grinning wildly. "What?" he snapped at his brother.

"Nothing," Quin shrugged, giving him a taunting smile. It was like they were sharing a secret, and I was desperate to know.

"Zev!" Alpha Rollen bellowed as my favorite guard entered the room. He wore a deep blue uniform and looked well-rested. If I hadn't known for a fact Zev's head had been busted open only a few days ago, I wouldn't have guessed it. What originally was an ugly cut was now barely a scratch over his eye. A wound like that would have taken months to heal on me.

Zev bowed and took a seat next to Rin, a plate immediately set in front of him. Quin shifted in his chair and stared down at his food, the tips of his ears turning pink.

"It's my understanding you were injured in the line of duty," Alpha Rollen said between bites.

Quin's head snapped up, and his eyes darted all over Zev's body. I could only assume he was trying to figure out how the Alpha had been hurt.

"Unfortunately, nothing permanent or worth bragging about," Zev laughed, his happy energy filling the room.

Quin kept his eyes on the Alpha, and I could scent his worry rising in the air.

I leaned in and whispered as quietly as I could, "That scratch over his eye and a few bruises."

Quin gave me a shy smile and mouthed a quick *'thanks'* before turning his longing gaze back to the tall Alpha.

"What do you have planned today, Omega?" Rin asked as he loaded up his fork. He went stiff, and his eyes snapped to me. "I meant Omega Quin. I wasn't calling you Omega. I was asking Quin. Not you. Not that I don't want to know what you're doing, I just—"

Rin stopped talking and dropped his fork. It clattered loudly on his plate.

"Someone call Beta Sami," Alpha Rollen yelled over his shoulder.

"No," Rin said. "I'm fine." He glanced at me, letting out a slow, angry breath. Then he abruptly pushed back his chair and walked out of the room.

I was so confused.

After how I had defied him last night, I just knew he'd still be livid, but he usually either ignored me or yelled when he was mad. Maybe he was trying to be polite for the sake of his father. Maybe he was trying to be kind and let it go. Maybe he was plotting my death.

Either way, I think I preferred an angry and yelling Rin to whatever this was.

The Garden

Rin

I WINCED as I thought of how stupid and weak I sounded at breakfast. Fumbling in front of my father and Zev over a fucking Omega. Emyanna obviously wasn't a good fit for me. She was distracting my wolf and messing with my mind, making me sound like a fucking fool.

I had fought in battles, hunted fierce beasts, and commanded legions of warriors but dealing with this one Omega was surely to be the death of me. Nothing in my life had been this difficult.

It also didn't help that I had barely slept last night. Too distracted by the warmth of the soft Omega lying next to me. I spent all night thinking about the fiery strength in Emyanna's eyes, her lithe body pinned beneath mine, and the taste of her sweet scent that remained on my lips even hours after I touched her. It took everything in me to not roll over and take what was mine, but I forced myself in place, looking at the fucking wall all night long.

She wasn't of age yet, and I wasn't weak.

I shook my head, trying to set my mind straight for the day. I had a busy schedule ahead of me, and I needed to focus.

Opening the door to the packhouse, I stepped outside and headed toward the center of town. I hoped what I was sure would be a horrible day would force the Omega from my head.

MY FATHER WOULD BE PLEASED with the plans for the festival honoring our fallen guards. I was sure of it.

I spent all morning with grieving families, ensuring my gratitude for their sacrifice was known. I hated sitting in front of a devastated mother, knowing I was only here because her son or daughter was rotting in a meadow somewhere. But I owed this to my pack.

The rest of the guards were ordered to spend time with their families before reporting back to duty, and I was pleased to find all of them on the mend. I visited each one to extend my apologies for making them suffer such a long journey and also thanked them for their dedication. I was very fortunate to have the allegiance of such good wolves.

It was well into the evening when I made my way back to the packhouse. Rather than head inside, I walked around the house to the gardens, wanting to enjoy the breeze and some solitude.

I was surprised to hear my brother's laughter as I walked past the small patch of lavender. He, Dara, and his maid, Anja, were sitting near the pond, giggling and chasing fat bullfrogs around the flat rocks that decorated the area. Zev smiled as they played, keeping watch.

"How are you feeling?" Emmy's voice caught me off guard, and I turned to see her standing under the shade of a giant spruce. "You seemed off at breakfast. Are you feeling better?" She captured her bottom lip between her teeth, waiting for me to answer.

I looked to see if she was mocking me, but she seemed sincere.

"I'm fine," I said harsher than intended, but I wanted to make it clear I wasn't in the mood to be teased.

She nodded and glanced down, a sprig of lavender in her hands. She ran her fingers over the flower repeatedly as if compelled. The breeze pulled her scent toward me, and my wolf growled with a deep longing. Her gentle mannerisms called to me, urging me to protect and dominate her.

I wanted to fucking ruin her.

Every thread of control within me frayed when I was around the Omega. My mind was constantly distracted. Always pulling back to thoughts of her fiery temper and tempting scent. The need to impale her on my cock made my fists tighten and lungs burn.

I took a quick step back, not trusting myself.

She wasn't of age, and it was grossly inappropriate to feel this way for a fucking pup, even if she was my mate.

"Emyanna," I said forcefully, suddenly angry.

She flinched and dropped the flower, pressing herself against the tree.

My anger stunted at her reaction, and I rushed to her, taking her hands—my wolf desperately wanting to comfort her. She looked up at me with those wide, frightened eyes.

"Emmy, I—"

The air around us shifted, and the wind whipped through her dark hair, making it sway and twist around her shoulders. Her eyes softened just a bit, just enough to show something beyond her startled expression. *Longing?*

Or at least that's what I hoped it was.

I dragged my gaze from the golden flecks within her eyes, over her pink-tinged cheeks, and settled on her lips. Those perfect, pouty lips. Slowly, I leaned in, expecting her to stop me, but she didn't.

Giving in to my wolf and the powerful pull she had on me, I pressed my mouth to hers.

Inhaling deeply, I moved against her, savoring the feel of her slight form as I wrapped my arms around her. My wolf rushed forward, and an animalistic need to take our mate surged through me, but I kept my beast at bay. Now wasn't the time.

Emmy moved her arms around my neck and pulled herself to me. A soft moan slipped from her throat, spurring me on. I parted her lips and dipped my tongue in, tasting everything she had to offer.

She was so fucking sweet.

Gripping her firmly around the waist, I tangled my other hand in her soft hair and deepened the kiss. I devoured her with a rough intensity I couldn't stop, and she melted into me, allowing me to dominate her mouth, completely yielding to her Alpha. My cock thickened, and muscles tensed as her arousal bloomed, the scent of slick hitting my nose.

I pulled back, gasping for air. I couldn't think straight. Emmy's cheeks were flushed, and she looked disoriented for a moment, but then she slowly smiled, biting her bottom lip. *Fuck*.

I wanted nothing more than to devour the beautiful creature in my arms, age be damned.

The Lavender Patch

Emmy

RIN LEANED into me and placed another soft kiss on my lips. He lingered for just a moment before pulling back, his dark eyes roaming all over my face. My heart fluttered, and my core twisted, desperate for more of him.

I brushed my fingertips over my lips, wanting him to kiss me again, wanting him to praise and love me, needing him to tell me he didn't wish I were my sister.

His expression darkened once again, and he pulled me to his firm body but stopped when a sudden squeal cut through the air.

Rin stepped back, and I jerked, whipping around to see Zev helping Quin up. The Omega appeared to have stumbled over the rocks near the pond. Quin's whole face was bright red, and he looked nervous with his hand firmly in the Alpha's. Zev was completely oblivious. I couldn't help but smile.

"What?" Rin asked, moving his eyes between me and the pair by the pond.

"Quin has a crush on Zev," I said, unable to stop laughing at the look of shock on Rin's face. "I'm sure this has made Quin's day. Look how pink his ears are." I pointed in the direction of his brother's burning complexion.

"Has Zev done anything to encourage this? Has he touched Quin?" His voice was loud and ridiculous as anger clouded his eyes.

"No." I smiled nervously, glancing to make sure they hadn't heard him. "Of course not. Zev hasn't done anything. It's just a crush. There's no reason to be angry."

"There's no reason?" Rin snapped, his brow raised and muscles tight.

"Yes." I backed up, his anger feeding into me, putting my wolf on edge. "It's just a crush. How can you be so mad?"

"Quin is far too young to have feelings like that," he said as if stating a fact like Omegas weren't normal beings with longings and desires.

I bristled at his ridiculous statement but didn't say anything.

"I don't expect you to understand." He squared his broad shoulders. I could tell he was on the verge of yelling, and it made me want to provoke him. So I narrowed my eyes and pursed my lips, knowing how much he hated it.

"The responsibility of caring for an Omega is not a burden to take lightly," he continued. I tensed, waiting to hear the undoubtedly stupid things that were about to pour from his mouth.

"Omegas are weak and emotional and easily manipulated by careless Alphas who only have one thing on their mind. Especially underage Omegas. Quin doesn't know what he wants, and he needs to be careful with his feelings."

His words burned, and resentment flared within me.

Crossing my arms over my chest, I tried to speak just as loud and firm as him, but it was still a whisper at best. "So I'm a weak, emotional burden, and you're just manipulating me?"

He hesitated for a moment, seemingly at a loss for words.

"That's not what I meant," he finally said, his anger fading momentarily.

Tears stung my eyes, but I forced them back, letting my fury envelop me. As long as I was angry, I wasn't crying.

"Omega's were not created to obey and pleasure Alphas." My voice was a little stronger. "We are allowed to think and feel as we please, whether you like it or not."

Rin's anger simmered just beneath the surface, his beast moving through his eyes. I took a long, steadying breath, fighting the urge to bear my throat.

Unable to take his silent disapproval anymore, I pushed past him.

"I'm sorry I'm not Sana," I snapped.

Rin grabbed my arm and jerked me back to him. "What the fuck does she have to do with this?"

I shook my head, not wanting to admit how wounded I was by one stupid comment he made days ago. But it had rooted itself in my head, reminding me just how unworthy I was to be here.

He didn't want me or choose me.

He was stuck with me.

"What does your sister have to do with Quin?" His brows twisted together, and his grip on my arm softened.

Forcing myself to look up into his face, I froze under his stare. His dark eyes weren't angry anymore but filled with something soft and sad. I could feel an uneasy emotion push off him through our bond, and my wolf whimpered.

The need to cry flared up hard within me and I jerked my

arm free, racing through the garden. I didn't want to give the Alpha a chance to force me to stay so he could insult me further.

Rin didn't chase after me, but I could feel his eyes on me the whole way back to the packhouse.

Quin's Bedroom

Emmy

OVER THE NEXT SEVERAL DAYS, I barely saw Rin. He'd come to bed well after I fell asleep and was gone before I woke. I only saw him at dinner. And even then, he'd give all his attention to his indifferent father, who was more interested in his drink, and an overly interested Zev, who talked to him endlessly about pack business.

In the mornings, I'd find myself clinging to his pillow, and when he spoke, the sound of his deep voice made my skin tingle.

Even though I spent my days with Quin in the gardens, sunroom, and roaming around the enormous library, I still felt lonely.

It was hard to be so near the Alpha and so far away at the same time. My wolf missed him.

I tried like crazy not to think about Rin, but I failed miserably. My mind kept drifting back to the feel of his lips when he kissed me in the garden and the awful fight that followed.

"You okay?" Quin asked, holding his arms out so his redheaded maid, Anja, could lace up the ribbons on his sleeves.

I nodded, smiling brightly.

I was looking forward to the festival for the fallen guards. I thought it would be a somber affair, but Quin assured me it was a celebration of their lives, and the pack always went out of their way to be happy and enjoy themselves. Doing otherwise would be an insult to their memories.

"They should have planned the festival for tomorrow," Quin said as Anja secured a gold bracelet around his wrist. It was lovely. Wide, smooth gold covered with a pearl inlay that shimmered as it caught the light.

"Why tomorrow?" I asked as Dara laced up the back of my dress. It was the same color and pattern as Quin's—deep azure blue, covered with beautifully embroidered gold flowers—and was tailored to compliment my figure. The pretty material fell just at my knees, and the details shimmered when I moved. It was so lovely.

"Tonight is the full Moon, and it's always wild," Quin said. "All the Betas shift and run around like maniacs. Not that I blame you," he teased, blowing Anja a quick kiss. She tucked her fire-red hair behind her ear and gave him a playful smirk. "I'm sure it's hard having your animal caged all month. I just wish Omegas could shift, even just once."

"Yeah," I said, not listening. The full Moon was tonight. I would be of age by morning.

My mind pulled to Rin and that kiss.

I touched the mating bite on my neck as my body flushed and slick started to pool between my thighs.

"Out." Rin's rough, deep voice sliced through the joyful atmosphere. Dara and Anja immediately stopped what they were doing and left. Quin stood firm, pouting as he watched both maids retreat.

"But we're getting ready. And this is my room," Quin whined. "I don't wanna—"

"Out!" Rin barked. Quin shivered slightly and rushed across the room. I heard him sniffle before the door shut behind him.

I glared at the Alpha, angry at him for being so mean. It wasn't necessary in the least.

He stared at me for a moment, then cocked his head, his tone much softer than I expected. "How the hell can you be so silent and defiant at the same fucking time?"

It almost seemed like a playful question. My expression fell, and I gave him a small shrug, not sure what to say.

"Emyanna." He cleared his throat, and squared his shoulders, acting as if what he was about to say was almost difficult. "I meant to do this sooner, but I've been very busy. I came to apologize for what I said the other day. I didn't mean to imply you were weak or a burden. I am well aware of how strong you are. The way you reacted when attacked in the meadow is proof of that, and I am sorry if I offended you."

I was shocked. My wolf purred at his words, wanting me to jump into his arms and feel his soft lips on my mouth and neck.

"What about Quin?" I asked, unable to help myself.

"What about Quin?" His voice was sharp.

Rin's brother was clearly a difficult subject for him to talk about, and I just didn't understand why. Quin loved to play and sing and read love stories. He was a sweet Omega with an innocent crush.

"You insulted him. Even if he didn't hear it, it was mean," I said softly, trying not to provoke the beast. "You said he was weak and emotional because he thinks a boy is cute. Why does that make you so mad?"

"Because..." he hesitated. Finally, he let out a deep sigh, and his face shifted. He looked wounded and sad, almost as if he was slicing open his heart to pull out the words. "Because he's all I have left of my mother, and I don't want him to get hurt. He's so sensitive and young."

The deep urge to touch Rin, to hold and love on him, beat hard in my chest. "Quin's not that much younger than me."

"Three years is a long time, Emmy," he gave me a pointed look. "He's only seventeen and still a pup. I'm guessing you're a very different person today than you were three years ago?" He waited with soft eyes, giving me time to answer.

"Yes," I whispered. "I guess I am."

He closed the gap between us and gently placed his hands on my shoulders. I should have pushed him away and forced him to grovel, but his touch was too good. Too perfect. I was powerless to his touch. *I had always been powerless to affection —I rarely got it growing up.*

"I know I shouldn't have yelled the other day," he squeezed my arms possessively, "but I need you to understand. After my mother died last year, Quin was left in my care. My father is useless. He constantly drinks to try to forget her memory, and while I may not be the most caring or understanding Alpha, I'm doing the best I can with what I have."

I felt awful. He was still wrong for saying the things he did, but I felt bad nonetheless. There was so much I still didn't know about my new family.

"What about Sana?" he asked, catching me completely off guard.

"What? Why?" I stuttered, not understanding why he brought her up.

"In the garden," he angled his head down to see into my eyes, "you said you were sorry you weren't Sana."

I shook my head, not wanting to talk about it.

"Tell me," he demanded.

"At the river," I blurted out.

He winced, holding up a hand to let me know I didn't have to explain any further.

"I think we can both agree we said some rather unfortunate things that morning." He gripped my chin with a gentle hand, tipping my head up. He looked so...sad? Maybe not sad, but definitely apologetic "We had an ugly start. Perhaps we should start over?"

I nodded, liking that idea.

"I don't wish you were Sana." He cupped my cheeks, moving his thumbs in slow circles. "If your fire is any indication of the strength the females in your family carry, I don't think I could have handled an Alpha version of you."

I laughed. "Sana was very fierce," I said proudly, tears stinging my eyes at the memory of my lovely sister. "She would have hated you."

He pressed his lips together to suppress a smile, but it was no use. I laughed as he did the same, and I liked the sound. It was deep and rough, not loud in the least, but I still felt it in my bones.

My laughter faded as his eyes moved down my face. A warm tingle spread throughout my entire body, and for some reason, I shivered.

"Emmy," he growled, closing the space between us, his expression going dark. His arms wrapped around my waist and his lips hovered over mine as he looked deep into my eyes. "*Fuck*, I want to kiss you." His deep voice settled tight in my chest, and my nipples perked.

"Please," I whispered, desperate for his safe, warm touch.

He tangled a hand in my hair, fisted the roots, then tilted my head back. He moved slowly at first, his soft lips fitting so perfectly against mine. He swiped his tongue over my bottom lip, and I gasped, opening up for him to slip inside my mouth.

I lost myself in his aggressive but gentle touch as he moved his hands over my back and down the curve of my bottom. He grabbed my thigh, pulling my knee up to his hip, and I could feel his growing excitement against my center. I let out a slip of a moan, pressing into him.

Rin rutted his hips forward, and my core thumped.

"Fuck," he growled, breaking the kiss. "I hate how much I fucking want you."

His rock hard shaft twitched against my most sensitive parts, and slick soaked my panties. I wanted him. I was dizzy and needy and a little stupid.

"Please," I begged. "Don't stop."

He let go of my leg and moved his hands to my hips, forcing a small space between us. "I have to stop," he said, his throat working as he swallowed hard. A clear look of disappointment fell over his dark eyes. "I won't be able to control myself if I don't. And we can't do this yet. You aren't of age until tomorrow."

"What's the difference between today and tomorrow?" I asked, feeling desperate to quiet the twist of desire within me.

"The difference is everything." He ran a hand through my hair and down the side of my face. His thumb traced my bottom lip, pulling it down ever so slightly. "I will obey the rules of the Moon and will wait one more day so that I can drink in your body properly and without regret. You are mine, Emyanna, and I cannot wait to make you feel it."

The controlled passion within his deep voice tingled my skin and twisted me tight. I felt I might die waiting, but I loved his desire to do right by me.

I pressed my knees together and let out a frustrated sigh, trying to ignore the drip of slick that ran down the inside of my thighs.

The Festival

Rin

IT TOOK everything in me to walk away from Emmy, but I had to. I was on the verge of ripping her dress off and fucking her like an animal on my brother's bed.

She completely consumed me. I couldn't fight my desire for her much longer. I needed her like I needed air to breathe. I had assumed my growing desire for her resulted from very little sleep and our mating bond, no matter how forced it might have been. But now I wasn't so sure.

Emmy dominated not just my every waking moment, but my dreams as well, making me wake each morning to a physical ache that only her soft body could satisfy.

I rushed down the hall, away from Quin's room. The second I got to my bedroom, I dismissed the maids, then locked myself in the washroom. My raging hard-on was killing me.

Jerking down the front of my pants, I fisted my cock and

pumped myself fast and hard, trying like hell to find relief. The feel of Emmy's soft lips and trembling body flooded my mind. I wondered how wet she'd feel with my fingers buried deep inside her and how tight she'd stretch around my cock. I couldn't wait to hear how loud she'd scream.

Fuck. The sounds I'm going to force out of her soft throat.

I let out a rough grunt through gritted teeth as I came into my hand. Leaning over the counter, I panted hard, hating myself for what she was doing to me.

Tomorrow was a fucking eternity.

Grabbing the nearest towel, I cleaned up before forcing myself to get ready. The festival would be a good distraction from the Omega.

"Rin." My father's voice cut through the air, killing my weak post-orgasm high. Jerking off was a sad solution to a problem only Emmy's sweet cunt could fix.

Stepping out of the washroom, I grabbed a pair of black trousers, pulling them on along with my usual dress robes. Dark blue and black with gold lining along the collar. Our pack's colors.

The thick section of embroidered black vines around the waist was held together by a wide leather belt. I pulled the straps along the forearms, creating a snug fit, then smoothed down the front, the material falling comfortably at my knees.

"I think I'd like for you to give the speech tonight," my father said, easing himself onto the foot of the bed. "I'm not up for it."

He didn't seem drunk, just sad. He got like this sometimes. It always made me uneasy. It was hard to see such a dominant wolf so weak and gutted.

"Of course, Father," I said, squeezing his shoulder.

"I heard from one of the stewards that you argued with your mate in the garden the other day. You need to get that under control." He clearly wanted his words to cut, but he just sounded tired, not meeting my eyes once.

"I've already handled it," I said, not interested in saying anything more on the subject.

"Have you seen your brother?"

I paused. It was an odd question. He rarely brought up Quin.

"Yes. Earlier in his room." I stepped closer to my father, staring at him as if his head might pop open and reveal his thoughts. "Is something wrong?"

"I saw him in the hallway on my way here." He let out a long sigh. "He's wearing the bracelet I gave your mother after he was born." He paused, staring at the floor.

Running my thumbs over my belt, I waited for him to continue. He rarely spoke about Mother. It was too painful. For everyone.

"Quin really does look like her, doesn't he?" he asked.

I nodded. "Yes."

I didn't know what else to say, so we simply held the silence.

Images of my mother filled my head, picking out only the best memories. Her chasing a toddling Quin through the garden, the wind whipping her long, dark curls across her face. The way my father used to laugh hard with his whole chest when she'd tease him. And the proud look on her face when I presented as an Alpha. She told me no one else would be better to care for Hund Valley, and I believed the passion in her words.

My father cleared his throat roughly, then slowly stood. "You should get going." His voice was weak. "Don't want to keep your pack waiting."

I watched him as he shuffled out of the room, disappearing into the hallway.

THE FESTIVAL WAS everything we planned. Food and music were abundant. Flowers poured out of the center fountain, collected in thanks to those that had died. And the pack showered the families with beads and scarves, thanking them for the sacrifice of their loved ones.

Everyone laughed, cried, and shared endless stories about those that passed. It was my favorite tradition at burial services, especially when there wasn't a body to commit to the earth. It provided a finality that was otherwise robbed from the pack.

Everyone enjoyed the endless food, drinking, and dancing, which went all day and well into the evening. The Moon shone bright, blessing both the festivities and the Betas that shifted, howling all over the village and beyond the border.

Emmy and Quin danced with a few pups, both laughing and twirling until out of breath. It was nice to see them so happy. Quin hadn't had much laughter in his life since our mother died. None of us did.

One of the pups spun wildly, stumbled, and fell over, scraping her hand. Emmy dropped to her knees and cradled the pup's limb, kissing it and wiping away her tears. It seemed to calm the poor thing until her mother rushed forward and scooped the child up. The woman bowed and thanked my mate profusely for her kindness. The poor woman was shocked when Emmy bowed in return to the still crying pup in her arms, thanking her for the dance.

It was so sweet and sincere.

"Sir." A guard moved to my side, commanding my attention. "A note from Casin." He handed me the folded parchment.

I broke the seal and scanned it quickly. Hector and his son

were only a day or two away, and I suddenly realized I hadn't told Emmy. It completely slipped my mind.

"Alpha!" Emmy squealed as she ran up to me. "Dance with me."

It was so damn hard to say no to that smile, but I needed to tell her as soon as possible, in case they arrived early. The last thing I needed was for their presence to catch her off guard.

"In a moment," I said. "I need a quick word."

She gave me a confused look but allowed me to lead her away from the town square. Pulling her around the bonfire and toward the temple, we stepped into the garden. Scanning the dark, gated area, I was happy to find it empty. I knew Emmy wasn't on good terms with her family, but I didn't know much more than that. I wanted her to have the privacy to react however she wanted.

"Why are we here?" she asked, looking around.

"I just wanted a word in private."

"But Zev is here." She pointed at the Alpha standing at attention near the gate.

"Zev is here to make sure no one else is," I said. "Pay him no mind. It's his job to be ignored." It was harsh but true. And he was damn good at it.

She scrunched up her face, clearly not liking what I said.

"I wanted to let you know that your family is coming to visit," I said quickly, not wanting to draw it out.

She stiffened and twisted her fingers together, squeezing them hard. The air around her tasted like fear and pain, and I was instantly enraged at whatever her family had done to make her feel this way.

"When will they be here?" she whispered, her voice distant and hollow.

"Two, maybe three days." I waited quietly, watching her try like hell to keep from crying.

"Why would you invite them here?" A few tears fell down her cheeks, but she remained calm for the most part. "I don't w-want them here." Her voice cracked, and she sniffled.

I wrapped my arms around her, feeling like shit. She balled the front of my robes up in her tiny fists, pressing her face into my chest.

"Emmy," I said as softly as I could. "May I ask why you don't want them here?"

"They're too horrible," she whispered against my chest. "They'll make everyone hate me. They'll convince everyone I'm useless and stupid." She pushed herself away from me, stumbling back, her face suddenly hard and flushed. "Why did you invite them? How could you do this without asking me? Why?"

I rushed forward and grabbed her shoulders before she could spiral into complete distress. "Calm down," I commanded. "I didn't invite them. I did *not* invite them."

The tension in her body eased slightly, but she still bit into her lower lip hard. I half expected to see blood seep out from the force she used.

"Hector sent notice that they were planning to come right after we left." I placed my thumb just beneath her lip, gently tugging it from her teeth. "And after this visit, I will *never* invite them to Hund Valley for as long as I live. Do you understand?" I looked deep into her eyes, needing her to know I meant it.

She gave me the softest nod, tears still dripping down her cheeks and her chin trembling.

"You are not useless, and you are not stupid. And I promise you, Emyanna, no one will ever treat you like that ever again."

"You can't promise that. My family. They will—"

"No," I cut in, making her flinch. "I am an honorable Alpha making a promise to my Omega. My mate. An Alpha's promise means so much fucking more than a few careless words of comfort. It's my word and bond, and I will fucking bleed to keep it." Her face softened, and my wolf warmed at my ability to soothe her.

"You are very important to this pack and to me," I continued. "You are...*good*. You are so good it's disarming and sometimes intimidating. And I'll be damned if anyone tries to convince you otherwise."

I wanted to say something so much more romantic or poetic, but I didn't know how. I was better with my fists than sonnets, and this was the best I could do.

Relief flooded my veins when a slight smile tugged at the corner of her lips and she stepped forward, falling into my arms. I rubbed her back and shoulders, trying to smooth her fear away. I would make sure her family's visit was short. I wasn't sure how but I'd figure it out.

"Sir," Zev said, clearing his throat. "I'm sorry to interrupt. But it's time for your speech."

Emmy stepped back and wiped her wet cheeks. She still looked upset. I wanted to stay with her but I couldn't. My pack was waiting to hear from their leader.

"Emmy." I kissed the back of her hand. "Why don't you stay here and take a moment to collect yourself, my love?"

I stiffened for a moment as the endearment slipped out, but it was true. With as much time and energy I spent trying not to think about this gorgeous creature, there were no other words to describe what I felt for her.

Emmy's cheeks went pink, and she glanced away, a small smile on her lips. "But your speech," she whispered, her bashful face hiding behind a curtain of hair. "I don't want to miss it."

I couldn't help but laugh at the sincere sadness in her voice. No one had ever expressed anything other than joy at having the opportunity to miss one of my speeches. The poor thing didn't know the gift I was trying to give her.

"I promise, my love. You will hear many of my boring speeches for years to come. You can miss this one."

Her sweet face lit up in a gentle smile, and she nodded. "Okay."

"Emyanna, I—" I stopped myself, feeling Zev at my shoulder. I had so much more to say, but this wasn't the time. "Remember. You are good, my Omega. You are a massive pain in the ass, but you are good. Don't forget that."

She let out a puff of a laugh. "Go give your speech, you jerk."

The Temple Garden

Emmy

RIN MARCHED OFF, briefly glancing back at me at the gate. He gave me a quick nod, his lips lifting slightly in one corner before disappearing back into the square. Zev's eyes cut around the darkness just outside the garden, watching over me from a distance.

Wiping my eyes, I turned so the wind could blow my hair out of my face. The hottest summer days were behind us, and while we hadn't been gifted a cool breeze yet, it still felt good.

I took several deep breaths and tried to calm my still thumping heart—Rin's words repeating in my mind.

You are good.

They weren't the kind of words found in sonnets or something young lovers whisper to one another in the dark, but they were still so lovely. He wanted me to know I mattered. I wasn't stupid or useless. *I was good.*

It was the greatest thing anyone had ever said to me.

Rin's deep voice boomed behind me, speaking to his pack with so much purpose. It was muffled over the crackling bonfire not far off, and I found comfort in it. The realization made me smile. I never thought I'd find anything about the Alpha comforting, but I guess the Moon knew what she was doing.

I let my mate's dulcet tones and the beautiful garden calm me. The moonlight struggled to break through the thick branches of the willow trees that framed the iron fence, but I could still make out a few colorful flowers. I was sure it was stunning in the daylight, and I made a quick vow to visit again as soon as possible.

Smoothing down the front of my dress, I turned toward the gate but stopped when movement caught my eye.

I froze, holding my breath and squinting into the dark.

A pair of glassy, grey eyes watched me from within the bushes. The hair on the back of my neck stood up, and I let out a shuddering breath.

Was this real or a trick of my mind?

My eyes struggled to adjust to the dark, but finally, the face became a little clearer. Pressed between two bushes, a round, white circle floated in the dark not far from where I stood. His pointed features and pale, waxy skin were just barely illuminated by the Moon. Shiny, slicked-back hair gleamed, throwing off an eerie sheen, and I swallowed hard, fighting the urge to scream.

"This isn't real," I whispered. "You aren't real."

I slowly moved one foot behind me toward the gate, then the other, each step careful and deliberate. My legs were like lead, and my knees weak, but I refused to take my eyes off that horrible, frozen face. The sharp eyes narrowed at me ever so slightly like they had a million times before, and a soft sob left my throat, my wolf desperate for Rin.

The crowd erupted into cheers somewhere behind me, and those frozen, unnerving eyes blinked.

I jumped and sprinted frantically to Zev. Flinging myself into his arms, I screamed and pointed into the bushes, unable to calm myself to form actual words. I could barely hear my own voice over the clapping and cheering behind us, but Zev jumped into action.

He pressed me into someone else's arms and disappeared into the dark garden. I looked up to see Ravana, the female Alpha who helped Dara prepare me that first night at the camp. Her light brown hair was down in soft curls, and she was wearing a pretty, blue dress. I melted into her strong arms, thankful for the familiar face. She held me protectively and guided me away from the temple and through the crowd.

The general chatter and laughter of wolves filled my ears. The lively music started back up, and I jerked, keeping my head down. I didn't want anyone to see my distress and draw attention away from the festival. I just wanted to disappear, for the earth to swallow me up, never forcing me to see anyone from Casin ever again.

I was somewhat disoriented when Ravana sat me down on a plush couch. I didn't remember walking back to the packhouse.

Feeling overwhelmed and confused, I pushed myself into the mountain of decorative pillows, wanting to hide. My wolf whined for our mate, and I could only hope he'd be here soon. Wrapping a strand of my hair around my finger, I twisted it repeatedly, trying to distract my racing mind.

It was only a few moments before Rin burst into the room, but it felt like hours. He looked frantic, and he jerked toward me before stopping himself, his eyes flickering to Ravana.

Zev rushed in soon after, moving directly to the she-wolf. I was desperate to know if he found anyone. If I truly saw that horrible Alpha in the garden.

I needed to know if Andrus was in Hund Valley.

But Zev's expression was blank, no panic or urgency, just professional and calm. It told me nothing. But right before I looked away, I noticed his eyes flash a vivid purple for the briefest moment. Then they returned dark and soft again.

Rin stood just next to the couch, his looming form tense and focused. He was breathing hard, his eyes trained directly on my face. I couldn't tell if he was concerned or angry. I didn't care. I just wanted him to hold me, but I knew he wouldn't, not with others in the room.

Slowly, his face seemed to soften as he took in my appearance, but he still didn't move. I pushed myself further into my nest of pillows waiting for him to speak.

"What happened?" he finally asked in his deep, official tone, turning to face the two other Alphas.

Zev immediately stopped his hushed conversation with Ravana and stood at attention. "Lady Emmy became very upset. It was hard to hear over the crowd, but I believe she saw someone or something in the garden that scared her."

He was being polite. He couldn't understand me because all that left my lips was a string of terrified shrieks and screams.

"I moved her here the second she became distressed," Ravana added. "No one saw us."

I wasn't sure if I had ever heard her speak before, but her voice was surprisingly kind. It contrasted wildly with the fierce and stoic energy she projected.

"We swept the garden," Zev continued. "Then I had my guards do a thorough search of the area, but we didn't find anything."

Rin turned his burning, red eyes to me just as the scent of

his rage twisted in the air, filling my lungs. "What did you see?" he asked.

"I'm sorry. I think I just spooked myself," I mumbled, too embarrassed to admit anything more.

They found nothing because Andrus wasn't here. The news of my family visiting had undoubtedly played with my mind, and I had needlessly frightened everyone.

Rin looked at my face carefully as if he wasn't sure what to do with me.

"Go," he barked, making me flinch.

Zev and Ravana moved quickly, shutting the door behind them. The moment the door clicked, the tension in Rin's massive body eased ever so slightly.

"Emmy," he sighed, his voice soft and welcoming. It instantly calmed my wolf.

He moved to sit next to me and reached into the mound of pillows, pulling me out. He sat me on his lap, straddling him, then he ran his hands through my hair and down my back, moving his fingers in slow, comforting circles. I melted into him, letting my Alpha's clean, woodsy scent swirl around me, calming my heart and quieting my mind.

"What happened?" he whispered, his voice rumbling through his chest and into mine.

"I thought I saw someone," I whispered, embarrassed. I pushed my nose into his neck, scenting him. He smelled so good.

"Who?"

"Someone...mean. From my old home."

"Did that someone talk to you? Or do anything to you?" His voice was so calm, but I could practically feel his wolf fighting within him, his beast desperate to protect me. It felt so good.

"No, he didn't say anything. It was just his face. I really do think I imagined it," I said, ashamed of the fuss I had caused. "I'm sorry. Are you...mad at me?"

"Of course not." He leaned back to look into my eyes. "After the news of your family, it's understandable you were frightened. And Omegas are—"

He stopped himself, thinking over his next words. I narrowed my eyes. "Omegas are allowed to be frightened just like Alphas," he said carefully.

I hummed in approval at his choice of words.

"How about I put you to bed?"

I smiled and nodded. I was exhausted and felt utterly ridiculous for the panic I had created.

Rin stood, holding me tight to his chest. "Come on, my love."

The Packhouse

Rin

IT TOOK a while for Emmy to settle and fall asleep. Even though she insisted she was okay, I could feel it through our bond and scent it in the air; something very real scared her. It clung to her skin and radiated out of her golden eyes. You can't hide the smell of real fear.

Once I was sure my mate was asleep, I ordered extra guards posted at the bedroom door then left to find Zev. I didn't have to look far. He was waiting in the entryway at the base of the stairs, his hands clasped behind his back.

"I'm not sure what she saw," he said the second I hit the bottom step. He knew what I was going to ask before I even opened my mouth. "I did catch some rustling in the bushes, but nothing was there."

I let out a heavy sigh, hopeful she was right and had imagined it. "I had just told her that her family was coming to visit. They aren't on good terms, and I'm sure her fear just fed into her imagination," I said more to myself than Zev, but he nodded just the same.

"Did anyone at the festival notice?" I asked.

"No, Sir. We moved her quickly and searched quietly. The party wasn't disturbed."

"And Quin?"

"I have three guards watching him, but I instructed them to give him space so he can still enjoy himself. I was about to retrieve him shortly and escort him back to his room."

"No," I snapped. I was still a little on edge about Quin having feelings for the Alpha, even if my friend was oblivious to the poor pup.

Zev raised his brow but didn't object. I only trusted Quin to a handful of guards, and Zev was one of them, which was probably why the Omega had developed feelings in the first place. Quin didn't have many options to choose from, and Zev was one of the few younger guards that worked in the packhouse.

"I'd prefer you to stay here, near Emyanna," I said, trying not to sound guilty. "Send Ravana to get Quin. I want everyone in their beds as soon as possible. It's been a long day. Too long."

Zev nodded and set off.

Between my frightened mate, my emotional brother, and my father, I felt raw. I turned and marched back up the stairs, needing a good night's sleep. I just hoped Emmy's honey scent didn't keep me up all night. I was sick of staring at that fucking wall.

I AWOKE with the sun to an energetic Omega pushing her nose into my cheek. "What are you doing, pup?" I groaned, having not gotten much sleep. *Again.*

"Nuh-uh, Alpha," she purred.

She moved to straddle my hips, and I froze. Was I awake? This felt very real but also very much like a reoccurring dream I had been suffering for weeks now. I was almost scared to move.

She placed her lips just next to my ear, her hair falling around my face like a curtain. "I'm of age," she whispered.

I moved, immediately rolling us and pinning her small body beneath mine. Her nightdress pulled up a bit from the motion, flashing her tiny, satin undergarments. My wolf was wide awake and ready to fight a fucking bear with the amount of electric energy radiating through me.

Emmy lifted her hips slightly and bit her bottom lip. I wanted to suck it out of her mouth. So I did.

I took her kiss with rough, needy movements, pressing my body firmly against hers. She moaned against my tongue, sending vibrations right to my groin. My dick twitched, growing thick, and she gasped, wrapping her legs around my waist.

I needed to slow down. She was inexperienced, and I didn't want to hurt her, but I couldn't stop. Her sweet scent and soft skin lit me up with a frantic desire I had never felt before.

Everything else in my life suddenly felt like a distraction. The only thing that mattered was making the gorgeous creature beneath me feel indescribably good. I wanted to spread her wide, fill her up, and love her endlessly.

I rolled my hips forward as I sucked the tongue out of her mouth, pressing my cock against her wet heat.

"Emmy," I growled against her throat, nipping at my mating bite.

"Alpha," she gasped as I rolled my hips again, pressing my thick shaft against her soaked satin garments. The smell of her slick made my mouth water and my balls taut. My wolf was desperate to feel her come on my cock.

I needed to be inside her now.

I needed to claim her.

I needed to touch her, fuck her, love her.

"Please," she whispered, arching her breasts up into me. "Take me."

Grabbing the hem of her nightdress, I slowly pulled it up. I forced myself to go slow, trying to regain control. My deliberately slow movements drove her crazy, making her whimper and writhe. I fucking loved it. She spread her legs, revealing her soft pink panties, so fucking wet with her arousal.

I pulled the nightdress up higher, displaying her adorable little stomach, begging for me to suck at her delicate skin. And the curve of her breasts, so fucking—

"Rin!" my father bellowed as he burst into our bedroom.

Emmy jerked out from beneath me and scrambled to hide under the blankets. I couldn't stop the enraged growl that ripped from my throat. My teeth lengthened, and claws stabbed into the mattress as I struggled to stay human. I wanted to fucking kill him.

"Shut up, boy," my father said almost lazily, the burn of alcohol on his breath. "You have work to do. Your Omega will still be here tonight. Don't exhaust yourself before midday. It's not good for your health. Now, hurry up. The temple priests have asked for an audience with you. Lots to do today." He turned and left, leaving the bedroom door wide open.

Dara stepped inside the room but hesitated when she saw the less than inviting look on my face. She took a quick step back and shut the door behind her. The second it clicked, I reached for Emmy, but she wiggled away, standing up.

"Where are you going?" I asked, well aware of how desperate I sounded, but I didn't give a shit.

"I'm getting ready for the day," she said as if it were obvious.

"But—"

I stopped talking, knowing full well she wasn't going to let me touch her with her maid standing on the other side of the door. Defeated, I moved off the bed and walked very stiffly to the washroom.

* * *

Once dressed and out the door, I spent my entire day thinking about the second I could return to my Omega.

I attended a meeting at the temple where a few priests asked for my input on things I couldn't remember. I met with some town merchants where they asked questions I couldn't think to answer. And I stopped at the guards' station house to oversee the new recruits, where they spoke to me about things I wasn't listening to.

I needed to get home and claim my mate.

I needed to feel her tight cunt stretched around my cock and feel her sweet breath in my face as she begged me to let her come.

The moment my day came to an end, I practically ran to the packhouse.

I fumbled to open the front door then ran up the stairs, taking the steps three at a time. Zev stood on the landing, waiting to talk to me, but I completely ignored him, rushing down the hallway. I prayed Emmy was in our room and was hopeful when I spotted Dara in the hallway to my bedroom.

"Beta Dara," I stopped her, knowing how out of sorts I sounded but not giving a shit. "Emyanna doesn't need anything else tonight. You can retire for the evening."

"But..." she held out what looked to be Emmy's night-gown, and I snatched it from her.

"Thank you and good night," I said, not waiting for her to respond. Once in front of our bedroom door, I stopped to address the guard. "No one is to enter my chambers tonight. Do you understand?"

"Yes, Sir," the young guard said, standing to attention.

"I'm serious." I needed him to understand my urgency. "If my father wants to speak with me, if he comes near this door, kill him."

The guard jerked slightly, then turned his head to look me in the eye. He opened his mouth to speak but hesitated, a look of confusion and panic on his face.

"Do you understand?" I asked in a purposefully harsh tone.

"Yuh-yes, Sir," he said, a little unsure.

"Good."

I ripped open the bedroom door and froze when I saw Quin sitting on the bed with Emmy, giggling. I groaned, unable to help myself.

"Quin, I love you, but get the fuck out!" I yelled, my impatience getting the better of me. I tried to keep from sounding angry, I didn't want him to cry, but I needed him gone.

He looked at me with his big, brown eyes, confusion twisting his brow. Emmy chewed on her bottom lip, watching me carefully.

"What's wrong?" Quin asked. "You're being weird."

"Get out," I said again, grabbing his arm as gently as I could and pulling him toward the door.

"You're such a jerk," he whined, tugging free from my grasp and stomping into the hallway.

I waited for the bedroom door to pull shut before turning to Emmy. My wolf growled, and my cock thickened.

I needed her now.

The Bedroom

Emmy

RIN WAS FERAL, his eyes darting all over my face and body in a wild, possessive manner. My wolf preened at being his sole focus and desire, all that muscle and power directed at me.

I shifted onto my knees, and his eyes followed my movements as if stalking prey. It made me feel vulnerable and wanted and a little frightened. It was thrilling.

"Don't hurt me." I gave him a slight smile, only half-serious. I knew he wouldn't, but my heart still thundered in my chest.

He shook his head gently and moved toward me, prowling slowly up the bed. "I promise, little Omega. I won't hurt you." He crawled over my body, pushing me onto my back. "I won't hurt you, my love," he whispered before falling over me and jerking down my collar. His hands were so strong and forceful, pulling at the fabric of my dress, but his lips were soft.

He slowly dragged his tongue and teeth over his mating

bite. A swift jolt of electricity shot through my body straight to my core, instantly filling me with a painful need. I pressed my legs together at the sensation and moaned. Rin made me feel things I never knew were possible. It was terrifying and exciting, and I wanted more.

I pulled him closer, my wolf a mess of submissive desire. I wanted to lay myself open and let Rin have his way. I wanted him to use me, fill me, love me.

Channeling my fingers through his thick, wavy hair, I tugged at the roots as he bit down, piercing my flesh ever so slightly. His chest rumbled as he sucked hard at my skin, leaving a dark mark at the swell of my cleavage.

"Fuck, Emmy..." His voice deepened.

He suddenly moved, yanking his shirt off in one swift movement.

He had slept shirtless next to me every night since arriving at Hund Valley, but I never let myself truly look at him. He was so powerful—glowing, tan skin over firm muscles and a defined v-shape with a tapered trail of dark hair that disappeared under his waistband. I swallowed hard, knowing I'd finally see what it led to.

"Do you want something, little Omega?" he asked in his sexy, rough voice, smirking at my obvious ogling of his body.

I laid back against the plush bedspread and smiled sweetly up at him. "I want you to touch me," I whispered. I had no idea where my confidence was coming from, but I loved the look on his face as I spoke.

His eyes flashed mischievously as he licked his lips, his tongue brushing slow and wet. He grabbed the hem of my dress, slowly dragging the fabric up my thighs and over my belly. He let out a deep growl as it moved up over my breasts, the palms of his rough hands brushing my nipples.

He flung my dress away, and I expected him to touch me, to drop down over my body and devour me like the animal I knew he was, but he didn't. Instead, he steadied himself on his forearms, hovering carefully over me. His firm chest grazed my nipples, making them tighten even more.

Slowly, he leaned down and kissed me with so much care and purpose; it took my breath away. His lips were slow and sensual, carefully tasting every surface of my mouth. It was surprisingly gentle and passionate, and I felt so safe and loved as my body burned hotter and tighter, demanding more of my Alpha.

"You are mine," he growled against my lips. "No one fucking touches you. This sweet, little body is mine."

"Yes," I spoke as loudly as I could, but it was still a breathy, desperate whisper.

"These lips will never touch anyone else," he moaned, moving from my mouth and down my neck, leaving gentle kisses in his wake. He positioned himself at my breasts and licked over my pert buds. "These tits are mine."

I nodded wordlessly as something deep inside me twisted, making my skin flash with greedy lust. I threaded my fingers in his hair and held him to me. He sucked at my breasts, pulling as much flesh as he could into his mouth, licking and tasting.

I was so distracted by the sensations he was pulling out of me I didn't notice him removing my panties until they were at my knees. Once naked, he sat back to look at my bare form. I felt exposed and a little embarrassed. No one had ever seen me like this before.

"Fuck, you're gorgeous."

He held my gaze as he stood up and undid his pants. His face filled with so much heat and desire I wanted to look away but couldn't. Those deep eyes held me hostage, forcing me to feel his intensity.

His trousers pooled at his feet, and I couldn't help but pull my gaze down his body to his intimidating length. It was thick and veiny and swayed heavy, with a bead of liquid dripping from the tip.

I pulled in a harsh breath as he slowly moved over me. I couldn't help the shiver that spilled down my spine as my nerves flared. He was so big. Would he fit?

"I won't hurt you," he whispered, kissing my lips and pressing his chest to mine. "I promise, Emmy. I could never hurt you."

A tremor worked through his body as he used every ounce of strength he had to keep from unleashing his beast on me. I couldn't help but fall a little more in love with him. He was fighting off every primal instinct within him to go slowly, *for me.*

Looking intensely at my face, he ran a hand down my legs and pulled my knees apart. Then he closed his eyes and inhaled deeply.

"I can smell how wet you are," he moaned, dipping his tongue into my mouth. My cheeks warmed at his words and my heart fluttered.

His hand moved up the inside of my thighs, straight to my core, as he continued to kiss me passionately. I gripped his arms, so nervous, as he slipped a finger between my folds. A warm sensation coiled in my belly, and I moaned into his mouth. It felt like nothing on this earth.

"This swollen, little pussy is so ready for me," he growled, watching my face with rapt attention.

I couldn't even nod, too lost in the feel of his hands. He rubbed and teased, circling his fingers up and around my sensitive nub, leaving no place unexplored. It was so intense. I thought I might die from the spiraling ache inside me.

He slipped his long finger into my entrance, and I tensed briefly before realizing it felt even better.

"So fucking tight," he growled.

Tilting my head back, I let out a long moan of pleasure as

he flexed his finger over and over again. Licking his lips, he rubbed his thumb around my clit, and I gasped.

I stilled briefly when he pushed in a second thick finger but rolled my hips, desperate for him to move them again. He obliged, intensifying the burn that twisted and tightened until my body finally snapped. A wave of pleasure crashed through me, and I threw my head back, screaming out his name.

"That's it, Emmy. *Fuck*. Feel that little pussy flutter around my fingers." He nipped my shoulder, still pushing into me wildly.

It was too much, too intense, too amazing.

I never wanted it to end.

The rush of my orgasm slowly calmed, and I fell limp against the bedspread. My face burned, and I immediately moved to hide behind my hands, unable to look Rin in the eyes.

What had he done to me?

I heard a deep chuckle and peeked out.

Rin removed his very wet fingers from my body, then put them in his mouth, humming at the taste. It was so dirty. I loved it.

"You taste so fucking good," he growled deep in his chest. I tried to roll away to hide, but his muscular body kept me in place, nestled between my legs.

"Oh no, my sweet, little Omega," he said, his voice like honey. "I'm not done with you yet."

He shifted, positioning his hips just at the apex of my thighs. I let out a shuddering breath, grabbing a fistful of the sheets beneath me.

I was scared and anxious and excited and thrilled and everything in between, all at the same time. His heavy member swayed between my thighs, gently tapping my clit as he leaned in to kiss me.

I wanted this. I wanted him. But I was still a little scared.

He moved over my body, kissing my mouth, face, and neck, kneading and squeezing my breasts, thighs, and bottom. His large hands roamed all over, and I lost myself in the feel of his lips and caresses. The twist of desire flared back up within me, and I arched up into his body, whimpering softly.

"I love the sounds you make," he whispered against my breast.

His girthy member poked just between my legs, and I closed my eyes, prepared to take my Alpha. He grabbed the base of his length and moved through my slit, coating himself in my slick before lining up.

Very slowly, and with a restraint I could feel thrum through his entire body, he pushed into me.

I bit my lip as a slight pain pierced deep inside, mixing with an intense pleasure that made my legs shake. It hurt and felt so damn good at the same time.

Rin pressed his hips firmly against my body, filling me completely, then stilled, letting me adjust to his size. He was so much. So thick and full and hard. I had to give myself a few moments, panting uncontrollably, before nodding.

"You okay, my love?" he asked, kissing the corners of my lips and jaw.

"Yes." I continued to nod. "Please," I panted, "don't stop."

His eyes held mine as he slowly rolled his hips forward. The deep-rooted discomfort slowly melted away, and I felt light and tingly all over. Rin moved his hips repeatedly, falling into a quick, steady rhythm. He licked and sucked every inch of flesh he could reach, palming my breasts and squeezing my thighs. I moaned and lifted my hips, trying to move with him.

"You like that?" he asked, his intense eyes watching me carefully. "You like how my cock stretches you?"

"I...Alpha, I..." I fell into a wild string of filthy gasps and moans as he shifted to ease deeper into me, hitting something inside that made my eyes roll into the back of my head.

"That's it, baby," Rin grunted, snapping his hips at a furious pace. "Take all of me. Take that cock."

I clawed at his back as the coil returned, twisting me up into a sweaty mess of pleasure. My breath hitched as he hardened and swelled within me, and I shattered into a million pieces. It was so much more intense than before, and I struggled to breathe.

"*Fuck*!" Rin roared.

His hips faltered, and he let out a guttural sound that stabbed my ears as his knot expanded, and he thrust deep inside me, sealing us together. I let out a shaky yelp as another wave of intense pleasure shook me, making my vision doom while he throbbed and spilled his orgasm, filling me to the brim.

My arms went limp at my sides, and I mewled, completely overwhelmed. Rin slowed his movements to nothing, and something warm and wet leaked out around his still pulsing member. After a moment, he went still and fell on top of me, propping himself up on his arms to keep from crushing my spent body.

I was so sweaty and flushed and sore. Circling my arms around his neck, I closed my eyes, basking in the feel of my mate.

My wolf stretched out, happy and sated, and my mating bite thrummed with Rin's shared happiness.

We were finally truly mated, connected, bonded.

We were one.

The Bed

Rin

ONCE MY KNOT WENT DOWN, I moved to roll off Emmy, but she clung to me, forcing me still.

"Don't go," she whispered. "Stay inside me. Just for a little longer, please."

I settled back over her, thrilled to give in to her request. My still hard cock shifted deep inside her warm, wet body, and she let out a throaty hum. Her hair was messy, and her eyes were blown out with a slaked passion.

I leaned down and kissed her gently, getting lost in her sweet breath. Tracing her lips with my tongue, I dipped into her delicious mouth, allowing the feel of her soft body to consume me again.

"You did so good, my Omega," I whispered. "So perfect, my love."

"I was good?" she whimpered, spread wide with my thickening cock buried deep inside her.

"So fucking good," I growled, grinding deep insider her.

She smiled brightly and sighed as I kissed my mating bite, ready to feast on her again.

I WAS SHOCKED when the sun rose, pouring crisp light through the windows. We had stayed up all night, talking, laughing, and fucking endlessly. I hadn't slept at all, but I felt like I could climb a fucking mountain.

"Sir." Zev's voice drifted in through the door. I didn't meet him at the station house like I do every morning, and he was probably here to collect me.

"Don't go," Emmy whispered, a firm pout set on her perfect lips as she snuggled deeper into my side.

"I don't want to. But I have to." I returned a sad pout to her needy one.

"Sir?" Zev said a little louder, hesitation clear in his voice.

"If you loved me, you'd kill him and lay in bed with me all day," Emmy whispered, giving me a wide smile.

"He's the only wolf here with any value," I snorted. "We'd all be dead without him."

"I can hear you in there," Zev yelled. "Are you coming out?"

"Are you?" Emmy asked, biting her bottom lip and doing a poor job of stifling a giggle.

"I think I have to." I hated that I had to leave the bed and her with it. I could waste the rest of my life wrapped up in her thighs, never leaving this room.

"If he comes in here, will he pull you out of bed by your ankles? Scold you for being a bad Alpha?" she teased.

"Sir?"

"I don't know," I smiled, still very uninterested in getting up. "Let's find out."

The door opened very slowly, and Emmy's face broke out into the biggest smile like the most incredible thing on earth had just happened. "He's here," she squealed quietly, wrapping the blanket tightly around herself.

I sat up and straightened my face. "Zev!" My voice was stern and angry. He froze in the doorway, his eyes scanning the room. "What the hell do you think you're doing?"

He looked right through my bullshit and narrowed his eyes, not an ounce of amusement on his face.

"I'll be out soon," I said, waving him off. He gave me a quick nod before shutting the door behind him. "I have to go." I kissed Emmy's lips before reluctantly pulling myself out of bed.

"Stay with me," she whispered from inside her little nest, only her beautiful face peeking out. "What if I gave you something worth staying for?" she asked coyly.

"There is nothing left in me to give," I laughed at the insatiable creature before me. "You took it all, woman!" I grabbed my clothes and pulled them on, not bothering to wash. I wanted to smell my Omega on my skin all day.

"Fine," she huffed. "Leave me. Abandon me in my moment of need."

"I intend to," I smirked, kissing her temple before heading out.

"Sir." Zev was all business the second the door clicked behind me. "We have a problem."

I groaned. "Of course we do."

Quin's Bedroom

Rin

I STEPPED into Quin's bedroom, bracing myself to deal with whatever had upset him this time.

My heart seized at the sight of my baby brother. He sat on the floor against the wall, crying. His small frame shook, and his face was buried in his maid's neck as she gently stroked his curly hair, humming softly.

He cried easily, too sensitive for his own good, but it always killed me just as much as it annoyed me. I was just hopeful whatever had troubled him this time would be easy to fix. I had a lot to do today.

"Beta Anja," I said, giving the maid a quick nod. She tilted her head in my direction but didn't pull away from the trembling Omega to give a proper bow. I was thankful. Quin needed the comfort more than I needed the formality.

"Omega, why are you so upset?" I asked, crouching down next to him. "Let me see you, pup."

Slowly, he pulled his face away from Anja's long, red hair. I sucked in a harsh breath, balling my fists to keep my hands from shaking.

Quin's face was battered and bruised. His lips were busted, he had a puffy cut over one eye, and deep, swollen bruises covered one side of his jaw. His whole body shook as he looked at me with pure desperation.

My eyes moved over his skinny body, taking in the black and blue marks on his wrists and arms. They were so dark, like his attacker was trying to break his bones. I heard a growl push through Zev's throat, and I turned to look at him.

"I had no idea, Rin. I didn't know. I just thought he was upset." Zev's usually light expression was tight and hard, and his knuckles white. "I didn't see him properly before coming to get you."

I nodded and looked back at Quin. "What happened?" I tried to sound calm, but I could tell from how he trembled that I was anything but.

"F-father," he said barely above a whisper.

"Our father did this to you!" I yelled.

Quin flinched hard and pushed himself back into Anja's hair, sobbing uncontrollably. He didn't have to repeat it. I knew he was telling the truth.

I just didn't want to believe it.

Our father was never a gentle Alpha, but he was always careful with Quin. However, the old wolf had been spiraling more out of control lately, even challenging me on a few occasions over the last year, resulting in more than one fistfight where I tried my damndest not to hurt the aged Alpha. But it was getting worse. He was provoked far too easily, swinging wildly between depression, rage, and indifference.

I just never thought he'd go after Quin. My brother was so small and fragile. Anyone willing to touch an Omega in anger didn't deserve to live.

Swallowing down what I could of my rage, I tried to stay calm. I'd be able to satisfy my fury soon enough.

"Quin," I whispered, forcing my wolf to back off. "Why did he do this to you? What happened?"

"He, he told me," Quin stuttered through his tears. "He told me he was giving me away. He arranged a mate, mating. I said I didn't want to go. Please, Rin!" he yelled, heaving between choked sobs. "Don't make me go!"

"You aren't going anywhere," I said with a fierce certainty. I simply couldn't understand what my father was thinking. He wasn't even of age yet.

Quin nodded but kept crying, clinging to Anja.

Standing, I turned to Zev, struggling to keep my wolf from taking over; my beast desperately wanted to hunt down my father and rip him to pieces.

I could see it on Zev's face too. He couldn't even look at me. His fierce purple eyes still focused on the broken Omega crumpled on the floor behind me. The odd color of his eyes always changed to a violent shade when he struggled to contain his rage.

"Zev."

His eyes stayed fixed on Quin.

"Zev!"

He snapped to me, his breathing suddenly harsh and the vein in his neck thumping hard. I couldn't send him to find my father. The Alpha in front of me was lost to his wolf, the beast practically begging for blood. I was amazed he had managed not to shift.

"Stay here with Quin. Do not leave this room," I ordered, not waiting for him to respond, then I rushed into the hallway. I moved toward Ravana, stationed just across from Quin's door. "Find my father. I need to know where he is now."

She nodded and disappeared.

Anja slowly edged out of Quin's room, shutting the door behind her.

"I thought you were off this morning, Beta Anja. The full Moon was last night. Did you not shift?"

"I did, Sir," she said, giving me a full, proper bow. "But I wanted to check on Omega Quin. I didn't see him at the temple this morning, and it worried me."

"Is everything okay?" Emmy asked, walking down the long hallway toward us.

She had put on a simple, blue dress and brushed out her hair, but I could tell she didn't bathe. My scent clung to her skin, especially around the deep bruises I left all over her neck and wrists. If I weren't so enraged, it would have made me smile.

"I'm going to get some things from the infirmary." Anja bowed again and rushed down the hall.

"Perhaps you should go back to our room," I said to Emmy, hopeful she'd listen. "Enjoy the morning."

She scoffed and ignored me, reaching for Quin's door. I grabbed her hand, stopping her.

"Rin," she said, her brows pulled together. "What's going on? Is something wrong? Why is Anja going to the infirmary?"

I wanted to force her back to our room. To keep her from seeing Quin like this, but I knew that wasn't possible. My fiery mate would burn the whole packhouse down to get to my brother if she had even the slightest idea something was wrong. And I wouldn't be able to keep something like this a secret for long.

I let out a heavy sigh, defeated. "Quin was attacked by the Pack Alpha early this morning," I said, the bitter taste of my words flooding my mouth. She needed to know before she saw him, and her fear fed into his. "He's...hurt, and I need someone to sit with him while I deal with my father."

She tilted her head back, an intense expression on her face.

But the air around her wasn't filled with fear. It was filled with rage.

"You take care of your father," she said simply. "I've got Quin."

She opened his bedroom door, her voice instantly soft and loving as she disappeared inside. Quin's sobs intensified before the door shut behind her.

The Visitors

Emmy

QUIN TREMBLED and babbled out repeated apologies as Anja and I cleaned the cuts on his face and lips. He kept heaving and choking on his words, and we had to stop several times, holding him tenderly to calm his breath again.

I knew the pain of an Alpha's open hand all too well. My father was a wolf of few words when it came to making his displeasure known, but Quin hadn't been corrected or reprimanded the way Omegas sometimes were. He was beaten.

Once Quin's face was clean, it took me almost an hour to convince him to undress so I could wash the dried blood out of his hair. I was disgusted to find his thin body covered in bruises so dark they stood out noticeably against his tan skin. A few of his ribs had to be broken, and I was very concerned about a large welt at the base of his spine. It appeared the Pack Alpha had completely lost himself, and I was surprised he didn't accidentally kill the Omega.

I swallowed down my rage, knowing Rin was handling it. I clung to that; my Alpha would handle the bastard that did this.

Upon arriving in Hund Valley, I noticed the Pack Alpha's passion for his drink. It was hard to ignore. He usually started drinking at breakfast and went well into the evening, but I tried not to dwell on it too much. It wasn't my place. But now, the old wolf had attacked my family—his own son—and it was most definitely my business.

Too weak to build a proper nest himself, I did the best I could, creating one for Quin. Patting and shaping, I tried to make the space as comforting as possible. Nests were so personal, and I hated he couldn't do it himself. I hoped he would find some comfort in mine.

Tucking a blanket under Quin's chin, I moved slowly, careful not to wake him. It took forever to get him to sleep, and I needed to find Rin.

I nodded at Zev, standing at attention at the foot of the bed, before stepping into the hallway. It eased my mind knowing he would be standing watch over the pup.

Walking through the halls, I was restless and not sure where to go. Feeling a bit brave, I made my way to the Pack Alpha's study to find it empty. Everywhere was empty. It was as if the whole packhouse had been abandoned, and a chill ran through me.

I moved toward the main doors, trying to find someone, anyone. The deep murmur of voices drifted in from outside, and I pulled the heavy main door open, then froze.

My father and brother lingered at the bottom of the front steps, speaking with Rin. A dozen Casin guards stood at attention behind them, and the packhouse staff lined the drive, welcoming them to our home.

Carefully, I shut the door and pressed my back against it, breathing hard. I needed to collect myself, but my knees were too weak, and I struggled to remain upright. I couldn't fall apart. Not now.

Quin needed me.

Rin needed me.

I wasn't useless.

I was good.

Taking a deep breath, I forced myself away from the door, determined to open it and face my family with my head held high. Deep voices grew louder as they drew near, and I panicked, flinging myself into the closest room.

I huddled behind the door of a sitting room right next to the staircase. I was sure I had never set foot in the room before. Old, intricate furniture, not built for actual use, decorated the tasteful parlor, large bundles of flowers sat in beautiful glass vases, and massive paintings of old, angry wolves dominated the walls.

The main door creaked open, and the sound of heavy footsteps thumped, coming close. I slid down onto the floor and held my breath, my hands already shaking.

"Where is my daughter?" my father's voice boomed in the spacious entryway.

"Busy," Rin said. His tone was tight, and I wondered if he had found the Pack Alpha yet. "You'll see her at dinner."

I carefully rolled forward onto my knees and peeked out around the door. All I could see was Rin at first. He looked ready to rip someone in half. Then my father and brother came into view. It appeared my mother stayed true to her black heart and skipped the opportunity to see me. I was thankful for the small blessing.

"Has she been a decent mate?" my brother asked.

"Very," Rin said quickly, not offering anything more.

Edging a little closer, I caught sight of my father's commander, but I didn't see Andrus. I wondered if he came with them—if I did see his awful face in the garden.

Closing my eyes, I shivered at the thought.

I wasn't sure if I wanted to have seen him or not. I was either crazy or should be terrified. There wasn't much room for anything else.

"She has always been very obedient," my father said as if giving me a compliment. "A good quality for an Omega, considering she doesn't have many talents to speak of."

"Actually, I've found that she has a great many talents," Rin snapped. I leaned forward again, needing to see his face. "But I wouldn't say obedience was one of them."

My brother grimaced as if a sour taste stuck in his mouth. "I have no interest in hearing what my sister can do for you in the bedroom."

"How dare you!" Rin's eyes flashed red. "I would never impugn my mate by speaking about her in such a disrespectful way." He angled forward, not bothering to hide his rage.

"Come on, boys," my father groaned, looking bored and hooking his thumbs in his belt loops. His barrel chest puffed out. "There's no need to fight. This is a friendly visit, and I require a friendly drink. Rin, where is your father?"

"Busy," he snapped, his eyes boring into Davon's.

"Everyone here is busy," my brother seethed, his tone getting harsher by the second.

"Very." Rin bared his pointed teeth, daring Davon to make a move.

I shifted uncomfortably at the hostility that pulsed in the air, their clashing scents making me queasy.

"I'm exhausted," my father stretched his arms out, ignoring the heavy atmosphere, "and I am tired of hearing you two bicker."

I hated having them here. In an instant, I was that terrified pup forced down the temple aisle with my father's eyes boring into me and my mother's glare pushing me. I was useless and stupid and a burden to everyone.

Too focused on my thoughts, I didn't notice my father moving about until he spotted me. I startled and pressed myself against the wall. His eyes went wide, and a smile cut across his weathered face. He moved quickly into the parlor and loomed over me, trapping me on the floor. I pulled my knees up to my chest and cast my eyes down, too scared to look at him.

"Emmy! What the hell are you doing?" he snickered, crouching down. "Still hiding around the house like a frightened field mouse?" He laughed. His unforgiving eyes pierced mine, and I tried looking away, but he angled his head down, bringing himself to my level. I didn't say anything. I couldn't.

"You should have come out and greeted us formally. It was rude not to," he scolded.

"It's rude to tell her how she should behave in her own house," Rin yelled from the entryway, his muscles twitching with razor-thin restraint.

"Come out, mouse," my father ordered, taking a step back. I stood and pushed myself away from the wall, fighting the urge to run. I edged around the massive Alpha as he refused to move, forcing me to circle him. "Here she is," my father yelled, right at my heels.

Davon smiled and moved toward me. His arms held wide. I closed my eyes and prepared to endure his forced affection, but kinder hands grabbed me and pulled me away. Rin wrapped a protective arm around my shoulders, pressing me to him.

"In my pack, it's bad luck for an Omega to be touched by someone other than their mate," he said. I pushed my face into his chest, thankful for the excuse. He smelled like rain and rage. A blazing storm prepared to destroy everything in its path.

"Your rooms are ready if you'd like to rest before dinner." Rin's deep voice rumbled against my cheek.

My father yelled out to his valet to bring his bags while Davon stared at me. An almost unreadable expression on my brother's face. He looked angry or annoyed or sad or...*maybe all three?* I didn't know, and I didn't care. I just wanted them gone.

The Stables

Rin

I squeezed Emmy against my chest, saving her from Davon's outstretched arms. He let out an annoyed huff then motioned for his valet.

I didn't care for these wolves or the way Emmy trembled when they moved near her. I wanted them out of my house and out of my village, as soon as possible.

Emmy's father was loud, obnoxious, and came from a very different era where Omegas were seen as objects to be hidden, controlled, and fucked. Nothing more.

It had been similar here at one time but my mother, being an Omega and running everything for my father, changed our pack's views rather quickly. She could do anything she set her mind to, and I missed her greatly.

She would have loved Emmy.

Davon was even easier to figure out. The Alpha was a jealous, spoiled brat who was tired of waiting for his father to step aside or die.

I could sympathize, but he was still a fucking asshole.

Keeping my hands on Emmy's back, I waited for the Casin wolves to disappear up the stairs. It wasn't until they were gone that I noticed Ravana. She stood quietly at the back of the room. Her cheeks were flushed, and she was breathing hard, but her tight ponytail and uniform were immaculate. She gave me a quick nod then tucked her hands behind her back.

"Emyanna," I said, gently grabbing my frightened Omega by the shoulders. "Go to Quin's room and stay there." She opened her mouth, but I cut her off. "I said go."

I wanted to say it in a kinder way, but my patience was gone. Hector and Davon took it all with them. She leaned away from me, her eyes narrowed and her mouth tight. I pulled her into my arms and placed my lips just at her ear, whispering, "Do what I say." I kissed her temple. "Go."

She glanced around us at the various guards and the few staff members collecting the luggage, then gave me a quick nod. I gestured for one of the guards to escort her upstairs. Then I rushed to Ravana.

I didn't look back at my Omega. I knew she was beyond upset right now, and if I saw those sad eyes of hers, it would gut me. And right now, I needed to focus on gutting someone else.

"Where is he?" I asked as Ravana followed me through the packhouse.

"The stables, Sir."

The horse stables were a bit of a walk, passed the gardens, around the pond, and through a long stretch of trees. A few stable hands cleaned the grounds and groomed the horses like any other day.

The quiet breeze and blue skies contrasted fiercely with

the fire burning inside me. It threatened to consume every ounce of me that was human—leaving my beast free to satiate his need for blood.

I moved toward the stable entrance, but Ravana cleared her throat, motioning for me to follow her. She led me off the side of the property to the birthing barn. It was a much smaller space, reserved for when the mares went into labor. Its purpose was to separate the pained animals from the others to keep them from causing distress among the herd. It was an appropriate place for my father at the moment.

The burn of whiskey and piss hit my nose the second I stepped inside. My father's bare feet poked out from behind a partition. I could instantly tell he was passed out.

"Is this where you found him?" I asked as I looked down at my unconscious father.

"No," Ravana said quietly. "He was behind the main stables, in the field. I moved him here before anyone saw him," she paused for a moment, thinking. "Or at least I don't think anyone saw him. I can't be sure."

"Thank you," I said, crouching next to him and waving her off. I needed to be alone with the old wolf.

I stared at his face forever.

He was puffy and red, his hair stuck to the sweat on his forehead, and his eyes moved rapidly beneath their lids. He had stripped down to just his trousers and a thin undershirt, both soaked in sweat and urine.

How had he allowed himself to get this bad?

I grabbed one of his hands, examining his knuckles. They were bruised and busted, dried blood embedded under his fingernails—Quin's blood.

Pulling him up by the front of his shirt, I jerked his limp torso off the ground, shaking him violently. I fucking hated him.

I hated that he refused to lead our pack when our mother was alive.

I hated that he forced me to take over the second she was in the ground.

And I hated that he was still so fucking weak after all this time.

A piercing roar ripped through the air, and I could only assume it was from me, but I wasn't sure. I couldn't feel anything other than hot rage pounding in my veins. I pulled my fist back and brought it down into the drunk fucker's face, drawing blood on the first blow. Red seeped over his white teeth, and I hit him again and again.

I reared back, ready to continue unleashing my pain and rage onto the old man's face, but I stopped, my wolf forcing me to. This was cowardly. I needed him awake and fighting back. I needed him to know I was collecting the blood he owed Quin.

I let go of his shirt, and his body slumped back onto the ground. He let out a short cough causing a small spray of blood to splatter across his cheek, but then he stilled again. His chest slowly rose and fell as if in a deep, restful sleep.

Falling back against the wall, I let my raw anger tear through me. I felt useless, unable to protect my brother from the one wolf in this land meant to protect him. I couldn't let my father live after what he did to Quin, but I couldn't kill him either. I was a coward.

My wolf let out a deep, longing wail—trapped within my allegiance to my father, responsibility to my brother, and duty to my pack.

I was confused and enraged and lost.

I needed Emmy.

Quin's Bedroom

Emmy

I SAT with Quin as he slept, unable to take my eyes off him. His sweet, beautiful face, usually filled with so much joy, was purple and swollen and streaked with dried tears.

He was the definition of light, and now he was violated and broken-hearted. I wanted to kill Rollen with my own bare hands.

Zev let out a deep sigh, and I turned to him. His eyes darted from Quin's face to mine. "I'm sorry, My Lady." He stiffened, fixing his posture so he was tall and tight.

"What for?" I asked, feeling bad for the Alpha. He looked how I felt—enraged and sad.

He shook his head slightly and looked down. "I don't know."

"Rin said you grew up here in the packhouse." I turned to him, needing a distraction.

"Yes." He smiled. It wasn't as bright as it usually was, but it

176

still lifted his face, making him look more like himself. "My mother passed when I was young, only five. I met Rin in school, and we became fast friends. When I was eight, his mother found out I was living at the priests' lodge, and she insisted I move in here." His eyes sparkled as he spoke. "She was a good Omega."

"I'm sad I never got to meet her."

His eyes moved to Quin's face, and they darkened once more. "Alpha Rollen wasn't always like this."

"I know." I nodded.

I didn't know, but I had hoped. The idea of Rin and Quin growing up with that monster while they were small and fragile scared me. I still wanted to believe this was a misunderstanding, and the Pack Alpha would never hurt one of his young like this even if he did spend all his time at the bottom of a glass.

"Before Luna Lacy passed, Rollen was patient and calm. He didn't have the usual demeanor of a Pack Alpha," his eyes softened, and the corner of his mouth lifted as if remembering something sweet, "but I think that's because he never really wanted to lead Hund Valley. Rollen liked to fish. That was his passion." His face broke out into a wide smile.

"Did he take you and Rin fishing?" I liked the idea of little Rin having a happy childhood.

"Many times." He laughed deep and soft. "He'd take us to the lake outside the border, and Rin used to light a fire within his father at his inability to stay quiet. He'd find any excuse to jump into the water and slash around. Rollen would roar at him for scaring the fish, and Rin would insist the hunt would be so much better if he could capture one with his hands instead of a pole."

I let myself laugh. While it warmed my heart Rin had something good of his father to carry with him, it must have made his transition to the wolf he was today so much worse. He lost his mother, then his father.

Zev's eyes moved to Quin, and his smile slipped a bit. "Quin has always been very bubbly and sweet. He's very much like his mother. As kids," he continued, his eyes going dim again, "Rin and I found his cheerful demeanor quite annoying and often teased him for it. I didn't realize how much I truly enjoyed his energy, but now that it's gone..." he trailed off looking at the ground.

"Zev," I whispered, moving off the bed and toward the Alpha. "Quin will be okay." He nodded, his face stern and suddenly blank of all emotion. While Rin's anger burst out of him, Zev's was restrained and seemingly more focused.

"I know." He nodded, but he didn't seem to believe it.

"Zev?" Quin's strained voice snapped my attention back to the bed, and I rushed back to him. His expression slammed into me. There was so much vulnerable pain in his deep, sad eyes.

"Where is everyone?" he asked, his voice raspy.

"Anja will be back soon," I said, smoothing over his blankets. "Rin is handling a few things, and Zev is right here." I purposefully didn't mention the Pack Alpha. I'd let Quin decide if he wanted to bring him up.

"Are they—" He sucked in a harsh breath through his teeth as he tried to roll onto his back.

"Let me help," Zev said, moving closer.

He gently placed his hands on Quin's upper arms and slowly rolled him into place. It was incredibly inappropriate for anyone other than kin and personal maids to touch a member of the Pack Alpha's family, but Zev *was* family, and his heart was bleeding just as hard as the rest of us.

Zev adjusted his blanket under the Omega's arms and smoothed his hair down. Seeing such a big wolf caring for the wounded pup touched my heart. A deep blush covered Quin's ears, and I pressed my lips together to keep from smiling.

"Is Rin mad at me?" Quin whispered.

"Why would anyone be mad at you?" I was shocked he would even think that.

"Because I made Father so angry." He looked down, a few tears slipping down his cheeks. "I'm a bad Omega that won't help my family. My only worth is to help bind other packs to us, and if I refused to do that, there's no point in me being here."

"Is that what your father told you?" I fought my rage, bubbling like lava and trying like hell to burn its way up my throat.

Quin gave me a soft nod, not able to meet my eyes.

"You are a very good Omega, Quin," I said, sitting on the edge of his bed and taking his hand in mine. "Binding packs by arranged matings isn't something that's done on a whim. It takes planning and meetings and lots of agreements. And I know none of that has been done for you." I didn't know, but if Quin was meant for an arranged mating, Rin would have told me...I hoped.

I stood up, suddenly feeling very uneasy in my lie.

"Trust Rin, Omega," Zev said, his expression so gentle for the pained Omega. "He won't let anyone send you away from your home."

"I'm going to check on my father," I said, forcing a smile.

"Should I escort you?"

"No, Zev. Thank you. Please stay with Quin. At least until Anja returns."

Quin pressed his lips together, his eyes repeatedly moving between myself and Zev. He looked so smitten and excited despite the bruises on his face.

Guilt hit me hard, and the need to find my Alpha pulsed

through me. I hated thinking I had lied to Quin. Even if I knew in my bones Rin would never let him be mated off, not at such a young age. But it still scared me just the same.

The Pack Alpha's Study

Emmy

I WANDERED THROUGH THE PACKHOUSE, unsure of where to go. Not sensing Rin anywhere nearby, I finally decided to return to our room. Walking past the Pack Alpha's study, I paused. The door was slightly ajar.

Inching forward, I scanned the quiet hall. A guard stood at either end, moving their eyes up and down the corridors.

Pressing my hand to the study door, I slowly pushed it open, expecting one of the guards to stop me, but they didn't. Being a member of the Pack Alpha's family, I probably wasn't breaking any rules, but I still couldn't help but feel like I was about to get in trouble.

Stepping inside, I looked over the empty room. Two leather chairs and a sofa sat on one end with small serving tables, a few cozy lamps gave off a soft glow, and the walls held a few narrow bookshelves.

My curiosity gripped me as my eyes landed on a massive, wooden desk at the end of the room.

I was initially worried that going through the Alpha's things would be difficult, needing to move items carefully and place them back just so, but his desk was a mess. Piles of parchment, books, empty plates, and crumbled paper littered the small space.

I could probably throw half his stuff away, and he wouldn't notice.

Taking a seat in the Alpha's big chair, I sifted through the various stacks of papers. The sheer volume of torn and stained parchment was overwhelming at first, but I was thankful for the distraction. The fact that my father was napping in a room just above me kept me on edge, and I needed to think about something else.

I flipped through schedules for guards, plans to prep crops and game for winter, a few notes from other packs congratulating him on his eldest's recent mating, and I even allowed myself to scan over a love letter from Rin's mother. There did seem to be a lot of love between them at one point, and I wondered what she'd think of her mate now.

Letting out an annoyed huff, I rubbed my face hard, then grabbed a tattered book off the edge of the desk. I was prepared to give up when I found it—a stained letter stuck between the book's last few pages. The Pack Alpha had clearly written it while drunk. The words bled together, and the ink was smudged, but I could just make out what it said. It was a proposal to the Myphic Pack Alpha to take Hund Valley's youngest son. Apparently, Alpha Rollen felt Quin looked too much like his mother, and it pained him to have the constant reminder in his household. It was a messy jumble of words that barely made any sense, and it made my heart break for Rin all over again.

I swallowed my rising grief and anger at the situation and

flipped the note over—no delivery instructions were on the back or wax from a seal. I couldn't tell if it was just a draft or the first in a series of many letters. I groaned in frustration and laid my head down on the desk.

"What are you up to, my love?"

I could tell Rin was exhausted even before I looked up. The trace of blood on his knuckles made my breath hitch, but I tried not to react. He walked around the desk, then leaned against the edge, forcing a weak smile.

"Sit," I said, moving and gently pushing him into the chair. I grabbed a rag off the floor, and a jug of water off a side table, working to clean my mate's hands.

"Find anything interesting in here?" he asked quietly, watching me work.

"A letter to Myphic." I motioned the note as I finished up with his other hand. It took everything in me not to let all my questions burst out of me like a damn. Rin didn't need my panic on top of his heartache, and there would be time for questions later.

Rin looked the letter over, flinging it onto the desk. Then he pulled the rag from my hands and tossed it back on the floor. "Come here," he said, pulling at my waist.

I settled into his lap and rested my head against his chest. He was warm, and his hold on me was firm.

"Quin isn't going anywhere." He ran his fingers through my hair, gently rubbing at my scalp. "Don't worry about it, my love."

The knot in my chest unraveled, and I took a thankful breath. I didn't realize how tightly wound I was, but I knew Rin was true to his word. Quin was safe...*for now*.

"I don't know what to do about my father." His voice was rough and tired. We both knew what needed to be done, but neither one of us wanted to say it.

"It'll be okay, Alpha," I said, running my fingers through

his wild, dark hair. He hummed and tightened his grip on my waist. I wanted to make this better for him, but I didn't know how.

Rin's eyes drifted down my face, settling on my lips. He moved into me and kissed me gently at first but quickly moved over my mouth with a rougher intensity. He held my face, sucking, nipping, and tasting me. I whimpered low in my throat, letting him control me.

I was already so needy and wet.

He pushed his large hand into my hair and pulled. My back arched, and I pressed my breasts into his strong chest, desperate to feel more of him. This day had been so horrible, and I longed to feel something other than anger and grief.

"Emmy," he growled against my lips. "I need you. I fucking need you *now*."

I pulled away from him and slipped onto my knees, tucking myself between his legs. Tugging at the front of his pants, I gave him a dark, longing gaze. His eyes widened, and, for a moment, he looked frightened to speak. I bit my bottom lip and tugged again, wanting to make my Alpha feel good.

A sexy smirk pulled at his lips. "You gonna put my cock in that sweet, little mouth?"

I nodded.

Letting out a darkly erotic hum, he removed his belt and pulled off his pants. Slowly, I moved my hands up his muscular thighs and straight toward his thick, solid cock.

Rin tugged his shirt off then leaned back with blissful anticipation on his face.

I reached out and took his thick member in my hand. It twitched, a bead of liquid pushing out the top. Unsure of what to do, I hesitated. Sensing my uncertainty, Rin moved his hand over mine, covering me completely, then moved my hand up and down, showing me how to please him.

Once he let his hand slip, I gave him a quick squeeze,

making him grunt. His thick length felt so hard, yet soft. Velvety skin covered the intense muscle. I pushed my hand up, watching a bit more of the pearly fluid drip out of the top.

"Lick it." Rin's voice was so deep and sexy, instantly making my nipples tight.

Opening my mouth, I slowly pushed the crown past my lips. The salty, sweet taste of him spread across my tongue, and my wolf thrilled.

Rin gripped my hair gently, guiding my head slowly down this length, then pulling back up. "Fuck, you look so good with a cock in your mouth," he growled. "Keep going."

He released my hair as I moved my head up and down, letting my tongue explore every curve and vein of him. I hummed at the feel of his skin gliding across my tongue and hitting the back of my throat, making me choke slightly.

I pressed my tongue into the tip, and Rin let out a hiss, gripping the arms of the chair. His delicious, musky scent consumed me as I used both hands to grip the base of his member, helping me take him deeper.

"Fuck, Emmy," he growled. "Just like that, baby. Faster...ugh...suck it harder."

I did as I was told and spit dripped down over his shaft and balls as I bobbed my head faster. He thrust his hips up with my movements, chasing the friction of my tongue. I had never felt so powerful, controlling his pleasure the way he had done for me. It was thrilling.

Rin moved me back, and I panted, his heavy cock slipping from my mouth. He stood and hitched his hands under my thighs, lifting me onto the edge of the desk and shoving half the cluttered mess onto the floor.

"Lay back," he demanded, his breath labored and a dangerous glint in his eyes. "Show me what's mine."

I scooted back, shoving more papers and books off the desk. Slowly, I parted my legs and bent my knees, propping my feet on the edge of the desk. Showing him exactly what he wanted—my slick-soaked panties.

Rin licked his lips, then grabbed the hem of my dress, ripping it right up the middle, clean in two. Cool air hit my exposed flesh, and I shivered, so turned on.

My nipples were so hard, and my clit thrummed with anticipation.

Rin knocked my legs open wider and moved between them. Placing one hand on my knee and the other at the apex of my thighs, he stopped to look at me—at my mouth, my breasts, trailing down to my incredibly sensitive center.

His gaze made my skin tingle and pussy tighten without a single touch.

Slowly, he hooked a finger into my panties and dragged it up and down, brushing against my sensitive nub. I whimpered and prayed he wouldn't play with me for too long before giving me what I needed.

"You are so fucking wet," he moaned, slipping a finger lazily into my wet core. I closed my eyes and basked in the feel of him toying with my sex. He moved up and round my clit, pushing back into me repeatedly. Fueling the burning twist of pleasure building up inside me.

Ducking his head, he dragged his tongue over my nipples, then blew gently, making them tighten even more. A steady warmth filled my chest, and my body started to fall toward that wonderfully familiar sensation.

"Rin, please," I begged him, knowing how much more intense it would feel with him inside me. "Please, Alpha."

Removing his fingers, he grabbed the sides of my panties and shredded them, leaving me naked and trembling. He grabbed my hips and jerked my bottom to the edge of the desk, his fingers digging into my flesh in the most blissfully painful way.

Biting my bottom lip, I watched as he pumped his length a

few times before sliding it up and down my wet entrance. I jerked and moaned when he hit my clit then I melted into the desk as he pushed inside. My whole body flushed as his thick cock stretched and filled me so perfectly.

Rin attacked my mouth, his kiss consuming and rough as he slammed into me, setting a brutal pace that left me gasping for air. His hips snapped, thrusting relentlessly, making my toes curl and my body tense. I was already on the edge of my orgasm.

"That's right, Emmy," he moaned, his deep voice rippling across my skin. "Come for me. Show me how pretty you are coming on my cock."

One more deep thrust, and my body shattered. I thrummed and pulsed and spiraled through his powerful movements. My back arched and I whimpered, unable to stop the tears slipping from my eyes. It was all so intense.

My body started to settle as Rin kept pounding into me, his hips slamming hard and his cock stretching me wide.

Sweat beaded down the side of his face and between the grooves of muscle along his chest and abs. He looked so powerful, taking me so hard. He was beautiful.

His movements became lustful and sloppy as his knot formed, stretching me painfully wide and pulling another violent orgasm from me. His thick girth pulsed as he reached his end, and I gasped at the feel of his hot release inside me.

Rin dropped his head to my chest, rocking into me a few more times. A gush of warmth pushed out around his member, despite the seal of his knot, covering my thighs with each gentle thrust.

It was so dirty and messy. I loved it.

"Fuck," Rin whispered, pushing his face between my breasts and squeezing them gently. "The things you do to me."

Preparing For Dinner

Rin

IT WAS A REALLY SHITTY DAY, but watching my mate tip-toe up the stairs in only my shirt lit my world up. She was beyond sexy. The material rode up with each bounce of her feet, flashing the back of her still wet thighs. I loved the idea of my cum dripping out of her with each little movement, covering her in my scent all over again.

"What are you staring at?" Emmy asked as we stepped into our bedroom.

"Your ass," I smirked.

She glanced away, all pink cheeks and soft giggles.

"Can I ask you to do something for me?" I asked, pulling her into my arms. "Feel free to say no. I don't want you to be uncomfortable."

"What do you need, Alpha?" she whispered. I loved it when she addressed my wolf directly. It fucking thrilled me.

She set her plump lips into a gentle pout waiting for me to answer, but I needed to taste her first. I pressed several lingering kisses to her lips and her jaw before answering. "Don't wash up for dinner."

Her eyes narrowed at my request, but she didn't say no. I moved my mouth just next to her ear and whispered, "I want to know that while your asshole-of-a-father sits at my table, eating my food, his daughter will be sitting next to me with my cum leaking out of her delicious body."

Emmy gasped and put a hand over her mouth. "Rin, that's so dirty!" she let out a slight squeal.

"Is that a no?" I asked, hopeful.

"I didn't say that," she smiled coyly, pushing herself away from me and sauntering toward the closet.

My wolf thrilled as I watched her slip off my shirt. She had such a beautiful body. I loved the dimples at the base of her spine and the freckles that dusted her knees, but more than anything, I loved the soft curve of her stomach just beneath her belly button. It begged for me to suck at it, leaving dark love bites that would last for days. I licked my lips at the tempting thought, realizing she was watching me.

"You're staring, Sir." She looked at me from under her long eyelashes. "Go do something useful and let me get ready." She turned her attention back to the long-sleeved dress in her hands.

"Yes, My Lady," I said, bowing.

I grabbed my usual blue and black dress robes, that matched her dress, and pulled them on. Once ready, the robes swinging at my knees against my fitted black trousers, I stepped into the hallway, leaving Emmy to finish her hair. I wanted to check on Quin before dinner. I just hoped he had been able to rest a bit today.

I opened my brother's bedroom door to find Zev sitting

on the edge of the bed, holding his hand. They were talking and laughing. It didn't feel especially inappropriate, but my wolf didn't give a fuck and growled possessively, setting me on edge.

"Zev," I said in a quick, loud voice.

He jerked his head in my direction, but he didn't stand at attention or bow. He smiled and adjusted Quin's blanket. It was somewhat intimate and sweet, and I didn't fucking care for it. I turned my attention to Quin, not willing to say or do anything that might upset him. It was too good to see him smile.

"Having a nice evening?" I asked, trying to sound relaxed.

Quin smiled even brighter and nodded. One eye was almost completely swollen shut, and his bruises seemed to have completely bloomed, deep purple and black across the side of his face and wrists. A few ugly marks also peaked out along the collar of his shirt, but I kept my eyes on his face, not wanting to make him feel self-conscious.

"Zev was telling me about your first patrol at Stone City," Quin smiled.

I eyed my friend, praying this wasn't true. We did many things in our younger days as new members of the guard, and most of those things should never be repeated to anyone, let alone my underage baby brother.

"I was telling him about the fight you got into with those raiders over that lost chicken," he said, giving me a knowing smile.

"Ah!" I let out a grateful breath. "I wasn't so sure Zev and I were going to walk away from that one, but we lucked out."

"Zev also said you got to meet fairy folk! How could you never tell me?" Quin's face was all lit up, and relief washed over me. It was good to know that my father couldn't break his spirit, even if he did succeed in breaking his bones.

"I did get to meet some fae," I smiled.

Quin was so young when I did my first patrols, and most of my stories weren't appropriate for such young ears. I didn't realize that I never got around to telling him about my adventures away from home. I was simply too busy.

"Have him tell you about the Targon Elves we met at a bar," I turned to Zev, "but don't tell him about the hannoth." I pointed my finger and smiled. "I get to tell him that one."

Zev laughed and nodded. "I promise. I'll leave that one to you."

"Okay, Omega," I sighed, not wanting to leave him. "Need anything? I have a formal dinner tonight, but I can come up later or...I don't know. Sit with you tonight?"

"I'm okay. But will you have Emmy get me a new story?" Quin asked, pointing at a small blue book sitting on his nightstand. "I finished this one and need something new."

Zev grabbed it for him and held it out.

"I'll let her know," I said, taking the book and tucking it inside my waistband.

"She told me about a really cute one with a wolf and a fae that fall in love." His eyes flickered briefly to Zev, and the tips of his ears went pink. "Can you ask her to get that one?"

"Of course, Sir." I gave him a full bow.

Quin laughed. He loved it when I acted overly formal with him.

The formalities reminded me that I still needed to check on my father. I had Ravana bring him to his room and ordered his maid to leave him in his piss-soaked clothes.

He could clean up his own fucking mess.

I only hoped he was awake so I could beat the ever-living shit out of him.

"You two have fun, and don't stay up too late," I said, resisting the urge to drag Zev out of the room with me.

I shut the door behind me and headed down the stairs, preparing myself for, what was sure to be, the shittiest dinner ever.

* * *

I made my way toward the formal dining room, trying to mentally go over all the things I needed to do today but never got around to. There were always a million things left at the end of each day.

Stepping in front of the open dining room, I stopped as angry voices caught my ears.

"How can you act like this?" Davon said forcefully to Emmy. They were both standing at the end of the otherwise empty room, looking very serious. Davon was crowding her, but she stood firm and looked him hard in the eyes. It made me proud.

"You have to help me, Emmy." He sounded desperate. "It's gotten so much worse since you left."

I lingered near the door and listened, not feeling bad in the least for eavesdropping. After all, if this was meant to be a private conversation, he should have shut the fucking door.

"I don't have to do anything," she snapped, crossing her arms over the tight, cinched bodice of her dress. She looked determined, but I could see her clenching her fists repeatedly, the subtle hint of fear drifting through our bond. It impressed me that she could challenge him while so clearly nervous.

Davon looked shocked for a moment but collected himself quickly. "Who taught you to speak to an Alpha like this?"

"You did," she huffed, taking half a step back. "You talk to everyone like this."

"You never spoke like this back home. I don't care for what Hund Valley has done to you."

"You never listened to me long enough to know anything about how I spoke in Casin." Her cheeks went pink as her anger grew.

"Omega!" he practically yelled, making her flinch. "This affects you just as much as me."

"This is none of my business, and if you need help from someone, I suggest you speak to my mate." She moved away from her brother, her hands trembling as she took a seat at the long table.

"Talk to me about what?" I said loudly, stepping into the room.

Davon hesitated for a moment before sitting down across from Emmy. He pursed his lips, deep lines between his eyes as he stared pointedly at my mate. "Nothing."

"My father's popularity is waning," Emmy said, keeping her eyes on me, "and Davon is worried what that might mean for him."

Davon glared at her, and my wolf bristled. "He refuses to let me take on any of the pack responsibilities. His sloppy behavior and ridiculous demands are setting the pack on edge. Our family will be overthrown if he's not replaced soon."

"This has nothing to do with me," she said, her voice soft but firm. "You wanted me gone. I'm gone. Take your problems to Mother. She always adored you."

"I don't need your fucking lip," he snarled.

Emmy shuddered slightly and squeezed her arms to her sides.

"Watch it!" I snapped, shooting him a warning look and taking the seat next to my mate. I didn't want to be too far should the asshole choose to act on his anger. "You will respect Hund Valley's next Luna. Don't forget where you are."

Davon's eyes shifted to me briefly. He sighed hard, balling up his fists and speaking softer this time. "Our father is leaving himself open for others to challenge his position as Pack Alpha. If that happens—"

"This has nothing to do with me," Emmy said with an

annoyed edge to her voice. "I belong to Hund Valley. This isn't my problem."

"The rumors of the Hund Valley Pack Alpha aren't that much different from Casin. I would wager we have a similar problem, and it might be wise for us to find a solution that could work to both our advantage."

My anger flared, and I leaned across the table, trying to keep my voice low. "I don't know what you've heard, but I'm going to suggest you shut the fuck up," I gritted out, a wave of fury rising in my chest. "I sympathize with your problem, but it's *your* fucking problem. Not mine or Emyanna's. Figure it the fuck out on your own."

"Figure what out?" Hector strolled in lazily, his strong voice practically echoing off the walls.

"Nothing important, Father." Davon crossed his arms and stared at the elaborate place setting in front of him, his attitude firmly adjusted.

Servants entered the room not long after, bringing with them carafes of wine and baskets of fruit and bread. I motioned for them to serve us, despite my father's absence. Ravana pulled the main doors shut and took Zev's usual place in the corner of the room, keeping watch. It was weird not seeing my friend here, but Quin needed him more than I did.

Emmy shifted in her seat, pressing her knees together and bunching up the fabric of her dress. She seemed uncomfortable and not just because of our dinner guests. I leaned into her ear and whispered, "Are you okay?"

She glanced up at me, a deep blush on her cheeks, her voice barely above a whisper, "I didn't bathe before dinner."

I sucked in a deep breath, trying to control myself. My anger bled into lust as my eyes roamed over my mate's soft body, tucked inside her tight, silky dress. Her bashful mannerisms, coupled with the lurid fluid I knew was sticking to her thighs, drove me insane.

My wolf was all over the place, battling between rage and desire, wanting desperately to fight and fuck. I was reeling like a newly presented Alpha.

Clasping my hands together, I steepled them under my chin to stop myself from slipping a hand up her dress.

Shifting my gaze to Hector, I tried to focus on my anger. It was a better emotion to cling to at the moment, at least until I got Emmy alone.

"Hector, how is your mate?" I asked, needing a distraction from the strain in my overly tight pants.

"Fine, still broken up about Sana. Such a waste," he huffed, leaning back in his seat and rubbing his chest.

I thought briefly of challenging the old wolf and letting him know I was well aware of his lie, but Emmy stiffened ever so slightly beside me, the softest sigh pushing from her lips. I placed a hand on hers, trying to soothe her. Sana wasn't dead, but that probably didn't ease Emmy's pain. She rarely talked about her sister, but I could sense how much she missed her. It must be crushing not to know what happened to someone you love so dearly.

"Morana is just barely hanging on. It's so hard to lose a pup," Hector sighed.

"Two pups," I corrected him.

"What?" He squinted at me, his eyebrows knitted together.

"Two pups," I said again. "Emmy left for Hund Valley the very day Sana died. She lost two pups in one day."

"Oh yeah," he said, picking up his glass. "I guess that's true." He waved his goblet at one of the servants, watching with rapt attention as his wine was poured.

His indifference was baffling. My father was shit with Quin, even before my mother's passing, but he did care for the pup...or at least he did at one time. But these Casin wolves seemed to not give two shits about Emmy. I just didn't understand.

I glanced at my mate and noticed her glaring at Hector from under her eyelashes. She seemed to have a bit of her fire back, and it relieved me. She looked so terrified in the entryway when they first arrived. I wasn't prepared for it. She was so fierce with me that it was startling to see them take her nerve so easily.

"I'm so sorry to be late, Sir." An overly formal Alpha in a Casin Lieutenant's uniform marched in as if on parade. His clothes were meticulously pressed, and his greasy hair slicked back. I waited for Hector to give an explanation for the lower-ranked guard to interrupt our meal.

"I hope you don't mind," Hector said, letting out a loud moan of delight as a plate of food was set in front of him. "I invited Andrus. He and Emmy were close friends."

Emmy twisted her long hair repeatedly around her fingers. Her eyes were cast down and posture tight as the faint scent of distress swirled around her, her fire smoldered once again. I looked over at our uninvited guest, suppressing a growl.

Emmy didn't like him here, and neither did I.

"Friends?" the Lieutenant snickered as he took a seat next to Hector. "No, Sir. We were much more than that. Weren't we, Emmy?"

"What the fuck does that mean?" I asked, not caring for the way his eyes drank her in. My wolf begged to lash out, and I had to agree. There was a violence in his stare that hinted at something dangerous. Something predatory. And he was directing it at my mate.

"Emmy *was* mine." He let out an overly polite laugh and forced a tight smile. There was a biting challenge in his words, and my wolf roared within me. I had to hold my breath to keep him contained.

"I had laid claim to her," he continued. "She was meant to be my mate until the *incident* with Sana."

Emmy kept her eyes on her lap, not daring to look up at the leering Alpha. Her hands trembled, and she squeezed them together repeatedly as her pulse fluttered wildly in her neck.

"But politics got in the way, and we weren't meant to be. Isn't that right, Emmy?" He paused, just staring at my mate, but she didn't look up. "I was just thinking about the last time I saw you. You always did love gardens."

The Dining Room

Emmy

I SLOWLY LIFTED MY EYES, my heart thundering in my chest. Andrus tilted his head slightly and gave me a crooked smirk. His cold glare held a subtle threat that made my skin crawl.

"What did you say?" I asked quietly, too scared to look away. I had to see him, to know he was still in his chair and not lunging across the table to sink his teeth into my throat.

"The gardens." His eyes bore into mine. "Back home, of course. That last night, before you were taken from me."

Rin growled low and slow at his words.

"That wasn't the last time you saw me," I said carefully, remembering his piercing glare from the carriage as I left Casin forever. The same glare he gave me in the temple garden only a few days ago. *It was him. Now, I was sure of it.*

He held the silence of the room, letting it draw out forever.

Rin snarled, his fists so tight a drop of blood pushed between two fingers as his claws punctured his skin.

I held my breath, waiting for Andrus to answer me, to admit he had been here for a few days. I could feel it in my bones. I wasn't crazy.

"No," Andrus let out a quick snort through his nose, "I guess it wasn't the last time."

He reached down into his waistband, and I leaned back, suddenly terrified of what he was about to do. I glanced at Rin, my whole body thrumming with fear and panic. But his eyes were trained on Andrus, his jaw tight and nostrils flaring with each breath.

Andrus pulled out a small book bound in bright, yellow fabric and set it gently on the table.

My eyes locked on the offending object, and my stomach heaved. Memories of Andrus' wet tongue in my mouth and the unforgiving doorknob wrenching into my spine washed over me. My bottom lip quivered, and I swallowed down a painful sob. The tiny amount of courage I had coursing through my veins dried up and vanished.

"You forgot my gift." He narrowed his grey eyes.

I grabbed Rin's arm, unsure what else to do but needing my Alpha to do something. Rin's deep brown eyes met mine, and his beast moved through them, his body shivering as he struggled to stay human.

"Alpha," I mumbled, tears threatening to fall.

Rin jumped up, his chair flying backward as his fangs punched out. "I don't care for the way you're speaking to my mate!" he roared at Andrus. "What's this game, Hector? You bring this mutt into my house during what was meant to be a polite gathering, and let him speak so informally to Hund Valley's next Luna?" His eyes blazed.

Andrus leaned back as if basking in my mate's rage. My father quickly swallowed his food, confusion pulling his brows together. But he didn't say anything, concentrating instead on his drink.

Rin snarled at Andrus, his voice rough and full of violence. "Whatever you thought you had with *my* Omega doesn't exist anymore. She's not yours, *Lieutenant*. Out of respect and hospitality to our guests, I'll warn you now." Rin leaned far over the table, edging closer to Andrus. His evil smirk faltered as Rin's dominance flooded the room. "I've killed far more impressive wolves for much less. Don't fucking test me. Remove your eyes from my mate, remove yourself from my home, and get the fuck out of my village."

"Forgive Andrus, Rin," my brother said, holding up a hand as if it would hold my mate at bay. My father rolled his eyes and turned his attention to his food. "There was no offense meant here. You know how it is. Young love is hard to let go."

"I don't give a fuck how hard it is. She's *mine*, and I'll break your guard's fucking neck if he doesn't stop looking at her like that."

Andrus gave him a tight nod, clearly holding back from saying something. His eyes flickered to me before he bowed his head, submitting to Rin's authority.

"But I never loved him," I whispered, my voice struggling to break free. "I never loved him, and you promised me to him without even asking me."

Andrus stiffened, and the muscle in his jaw ticked at my words.

"I never once gave you a loving look or invited your touch or company," I said to the Alpha, keeping my head down. It was just too hard to look at him, but Rin's rage gave me strength, and I knew he would protect me. "I didn't want to be your mate, and I didn't want to give you my first kiss. But you stole it anyway." Tears fell down my face as a possessive fury burned through my bond with Rin. But he didn't speak, letting me say everything I needed to.

"You took that special kiss for your own, and I hate you for it." My chest heaved with each breath, and my throat burned from the strain of trying to speak through my tears.

"It's okay, Emmy," Andrus said quietly, his eyes sliding to Rin for a quick moment. "I understand." He gave me that disgusting, tight smile.

Rin planted his hands flat on the table and leaned over, getting as close to Andrus as he could. "Get out."

They were simple words but filled with the promise of so much violence.

"Rin!" my father protested, leaning away from his plate and rubbing his chest. "This is a friendly—"

"It's okay, Alpha Hector," Andrus said, getting up and smoothing down the front of his uniform. "I understand a wolf's need to possess and protect their mate. I'll go." He smiled at Rin before turning his attention to me, his eyes lingering on my face before walking off.

I grabbed Rin's hand and pressed it against my cheek, needing the feel of his skin on mine.

Andrus walked out of the room at a leisurely pace, without any urgency. It set my teeth on edge. I wanted to shove him out of the room, down the hall, straight onto the front steps, and out the village gates.

Rin snapped his fingers at a guard standing on the side of the room, and he instantly followed him. I couldn't breathe or move until the footsteps down the hall disappeared completely.

"Rin, please accept my apologies," Davon sighed, more annoyance than sincerity in his tone. "I hope you don't take Andrus' presence tonight as an offense. I really thought Emmy might like to see him. Clearly, I was wrong." He shot me a quick look that held no sympathy. "It appears I was wrong about a lot of things."

I couldn't deal with any of this anymore—my father's loud chewing, Davon's cutting glare, Andrus' lingering pine scent, even Rin's worried eyes. It was all too much. Without a word, I stood up as calmly as I could and walked out of the dining room. Grabbing the front of my long dress, I lifted it off the floor and ran down the hall.

I just needed a breath of fresh air and a few moments of silence.

After Dinner

Emmy

NOT KNOWING where else to go, I ended up in Quin's room.

I sat at the end of a settee in the corner while Dara and Anja whispered amongst themselves. Dara worked on a piece of beautifully intricate needlepoint, and Anja mended the cuff of one of Quin's favorite robes.

I read and re-read the same paragraph in my book about a hundred times. I just couldn't focus.

My attention kept pulling to Zev sitting in a chair just next to Quin's bed. He spoke in such an animated fashion as the Omega laughed and gasped at his stories. I wanted to enjoy his tales, but I was too restless.

I wanted to leave, but I didn't know where to go.

I wanted to be alone, but not by myself.

I needed everyone to stop talking, but I hated the silence.

Exhaustion swirled within me.

As the sun started to set behind dense, grey clouds, I

decided I needed to move. Trying not to draw attention to myself, I padded toward the door.

"Do you need something, My Lady?" Dara asked, leaning forward a bit.

I stopped in front of the door. "I'm just going to the library."

"I'll come with you." She sat down her needlepoint.

"No." I held up my hands, motioning for her to stay. This was supposed to be her day off, but my family's early arrival had ruined that for her. I wasn't going to take the evening from her as well. "Alpha Jacks escorted me here. He can walk me to the library."

"Why is a guard escorting you through the packhouse?" Quin moved to sit up, his big eyes flooded with worry.

Zev placed a hand on his shoulder, easing him back down. "We have another pack visiting. It's protocol. Nothing to worry about."

I didn't know if that was true, but it sounded better than admitting that Rin ordered a guard to follow me after I stormed out at dinner.

I quickly left with Jacks on my heels. The blond alpha moved slowly, giving me space, which I was thankful for, but his heavy feet thumping against the wood didn't help settle my nerves. The thought of hearing him stomp around the library didn't seem very relaxing either.

Making my way through the packhouse, I headed down the stairs toward the back east wing. I was so lost in the sound of my feet, followed by the guard behind me and his heavy rhythmic movements, I almost didn't hear Omega Karlin scurrying behind us, trying to get Jacks' attention.

I pulled to a stop, turning with the Alpha, and Karlin's eyes went wide at the sight of me.

"My Lady." He bowed. "I'm sorry, I didn't realize Alpha Jacks was escorting you."

"No, please," I motioned to the guard. "I'm in no hurry."

"My Lady, I can speak with Omega Karlin later," Jacks said, but his body still angled toward the small Omega. Karlin bounced on the balls of his feet, looking nervously at the Alpha.

"Jacks." I smiled, tucking my hands behind my back. "I must insist. Please. Take your time."

The broad Alpha glanced at Karlin, then muttered that he would be very quick. I turned away from the pair, trying not to notice how closely they leaned in to talk or how soft the Alpha's tone was.

Moving my eyes down the long corridor, I looked out at the storm flashing just outside the window. Thunder gently rumbled, vibrating the soles of my feet. I loved these kinds of storms. They were lullabies on hot summer nights.

A soft glow seeped out from beneath the Pack Alpha's study, and I paused. It was unusual for the staff to leave lights on so late, and I immediately thought of Rin. Maybe he was inside.

I edged closer, finding the door cracked ever so slightly. I could feel a presence on the other side of the door, but it wasn't my mate. Whiskey and beer washed out the scent of at least two wolves. My heart raced and wolf snarled at the prospect of being this close to Rollen.

Placing my ear next to the door, I pressed my lips together as the sound of overlapping laughter made me lean in. Angling my head at the crack in the door, I saw my father sitting in an old armchair, drinking deeply from a stein.

"How have you been holding up without Lacy?" he asked, taking a long pull from his cup. I rarely saw my father drink back in Casin, but I rarely saw him in general.

Rollen plopped into the chair next to the old wolf and sighed. His face was bruised with a few cuts along his jaw, but that was it.

Did Rin already speak to him? Surely a few bruises weren't the only penance he had paid.

"I'd love to say I've done well, but I haven't." A twinge of sadness twisted between Rollen's brows, and he rubbed his chest, looking nervous all of a sudden. "I lost it a few nights back and smacked around my youngest. I think I went too hard on him. It's hard to say for sure. I haven't seen him since."

My fists tightened, and the urge to scream thumped hard in my chest.

"Don't think on it too much." My father smacked his lips, looking around the room as if disinterested. "A good whack is good for growing pups. It keeps them in line."

I shook my head, refusing to think about my father and his preferred method of discipline.

"He's a weak one, though. An Omega." Rollen groaned. "Lacy would have tore me up if she were still here. She treated that pup like he was made of glass." He looked longingly at the floor before taking a long sip of the amber-colored liquid.

"You know, I struggled when Emmy presented as an Omega. But, deep down, I think we always knew she'd turn out that way. As a pup, she was always so jumpy and fidgety, weak as all hell. But it was still hard. We had no idea what to do with her. At least you had Lacy to help out with Quin. Omegas are just too much for me to handle." My father stretched out. "You know she ruined our true Alpha status. Six generations of all Alphas. One careless night with my mate, and suddenly our reputation is ruined," he said, looking pained to admit it.

I swallowed hard, forcing my body to remain numb to his words as he continued.

"Morana's father was so pissed," he said through tight lips. "Hated her for birthing something so weak, even insisted we toss the runt out, but she couldn't do it. She wanted to keep

Emmy. That asshole was always so hard on the old girl for it. Poor Morana."

"That's a hard one," Rollen sighed. "It's a point of pride to come from a true Alpha family. But still, you can't blame Omegas for being what they are. I just wish they would accept their purpose sooner and stop with all the tears."

"Don't talk too smooth, my friend!" My father's laugh ripped through the quiet house. "You forget that I knew your mate. Lacy was a fierce one!"

"That she was," he laughed, nodding in agreement. "That woman could gut you with a look." Rollen looked down into his drink, swirling the liquid around in gentle circles. The corners of his eyes fell a bit, and for a moment, I thought he might cry. "It's a shame neither one of my boys got her grit. Not an ounce of backbone between them. Rin is a decent enough leader, but he has no real fight in him."

"I understand that," my father yelled. "Sana was the only good one we had. Mouthy, little bitch and filled with fire. Davon will do okay running the pack, but he needs a strong partner. Like my Morana."

"You can't stand your mate, and you know it!" Rollen smacked my father's arm with a bark of a laugh, causing some of his drink to slosh down his robes. "Don't pretend you do, you old bastard!"

My father howled with laughter, wiping his shirt lazily.

"But you know," Rollen caught his breath and let out a heavy sigh, "that's what Quin needs too. A strong partner, someone that'll toughen him up. Help him reach his full potential."

I stepped away from the door, unable to listen anymore. Sucking in a deep breath through my nose, I released it slowly out of my mouth, willing my heart to calm.

Turning, I slapped a hand over my mouth to stifle a scream.

Alpha Jacks held up his hands, his dark eyes wide. "I didn't mean to startle you, My Lady."

I nodded, pressing my hand against my chest. My heart hammered furiously, and I let out a nervous laugh. "That's okay."

"Do you still want to go to the library, or would you like me to escort you to your room?" He tucked his hands behind his back, waiting politely.

"Library, please."

He motioned forward, and I led the way. I was exhausted, but I knew I wouldn't sleep a wink tonight. I needed something to occupy my mind.

I needed a good book and my Alpha.

The Library

Emmy

A LOUD CRACK ripped through the silence, and I flung my hands out to protect my face. Confused and disoriented, I rubbed my eyes hard and sat up. The room spun, my throat tightening. Moving onto my hands and knees, I heaved onto the polished marble, coughing and choking on nothing. Finally, I sucked in a painful breath of air, and my chest eased.

Where was I?

I wiped the spit off my chin then squinted into the dark.

The library.

I was on the floor in the center of an aisle of books. The shelves on either side of me disappeared into the shadows, everything around me still and quiet.

How did I get here?

I vaguely remembered opening the heavy double doors and stepping inside. It was unusually dark. A guard was with me.

How long ago was that?

The dense smack of a fist connecting with flesh thumped the quiet air around me, followed by a pained grunt. I spun in its direction, instantly regretting it. My vision doubled, and I leaned over, pressing my forehead to the cool floor, trying to steady myself again.

Two overlapping growls echoed around me, and I swallowed hard, forcing myself to my feet. My knees were weak, and a thin layer of sweat made my hair stick to my forehead. I was so hot and dizzy. Forcing my feet to move, I stumbled to the end of the aisle.

Another ripping snarl.

Something heavy smacked into a wall.

Books falling.

Muffled grunts.

Then silence.

Silence that hurt.

It was so thick it filled my ears and twisted the skin along my spine.

The slightest creak of the floorboards tickled down the side of my neck, and I froze. Holding my breath, I listened as hard as I could for any other sound.

Lightning flashed overhead, making everything bright and visible, then just as quickly, I was thrown into darkness. A crack of thunder made me jerk, followed by a consuming quiet once again.

Everything was so still.

The air.

The shadows.

My feet.

Nothing moved.

A chill threaded down my spine, and I darted my eyes around, wishing Rin was here. His Alpha eyes would cut through the black with such ease.

A loud thump bounced off the shelves just next to me, and my wolf wailed, raging hard in my chest right alongside my heart. I struggled to hang on to any semblance of calm.

My fingers gripped the edge of a shelf, and I crouched down, trying to shrink into the dark. My wolf didn't know whether to run, hide, or scream, and the internal conflict had seized my body.

I slowly peeked into the darkness again, tears blurring my vision, not wanting to look away but terrified of what I couldn't see behind me.

"Help," I said as loudly as my voice would allow.

Another bright flash of lightning and roar of thunder made me shriek. I bolted, my long dress kicking up with each hurried step.

I rushed down the aisle, made a sharp right, cut through two more narrow passageways of books, and sprinted through the corridor that connected the two rooms of the library. But I was turned around. I went the wrong way.

Standing near the library's back wall, I was nowhere near the main doors. Panic flooded me as I realized I didn't know where I was. I was lost and trapped. *But with who?*

The air behind me shifted and tingled. My hair gently swayed from a quick gust of air, and I spun. Swallowing down a whimper, I found only books that disappeared into more shadows.

A sob bubbled out of my throat as fear overtook me.

The thick scent of pine and smoke permeated the air, and my knees buckled. My body smacked into the floor as I choked on the familiar odor, my stomach lurching with each breath. I needed to run, but my legs refused. Sharp pine pushed its way up my nose and into my lungs, invading my body just like he did on my last night in Casin. Andrus and his snake-like tongue.

I shuddered out another sob and tried to stand, but I

couldn't get my feet under me. My body quaked as I dragged it through the corridor into the main room. Several rows of books blocked my view of the doors, but I knew they were there just on the other side of the room. So close, but so damn far.

"Oh, Emmy," Andrus' voice cut through the quiet shadows.

I pressed my forehead to the cool floor and sobbed.

The Alcove in the Library

Emmy

"I KNEW you'd eventually come here," Andrus said with an air of satisfaction as he walked up behind me. "You do love your books."

I forced myself to move, slapping my hands on the smooth marble floor and pulling my body forward. I inched so slowly, fighting my wolf's insistence to curl up and sob.

"It's okay, Omega," he said, his feet connecting hard with the shiny floor. He moved directly in front of me, blocking my path. Lightning cracked again, and the electric light flashed on the polished tile, making me flinch.

He was naked, his chest covered in blood, and black streaks of what looked like soot coated his hands. My whole body flooded with guilt and fear. Where was Jacks? Did Andrus kill him? Why did Andrus reek of smoke? Was there a fire?

"Let me help you up," he said with an amused lift to his

voice. I closed my eyes and prepared myself to endure his touch.

Large hands grabbed me just under my arms and pulled me up with ease. His fingers lingered, and he grazed the sides of my breasts as he pulled away. I recoiled and crossed my arms over my chest, my skin itching at his touch. I could do nothing to stop the tears from dripping down my face, but I did my damndest to hold back my sobs.

He looked at my face and let out a quick laugh. "Omegas," he pushed out a heavy breath of air, "so emotional."

I kept my eyes on the floor, watching the reflection of the storm flash and dance across the smooth surface.

"I heard you at dinner." He placed a long finger under my chin and tilted my head up. He looked so smug. "I know you didn't mean what you said. It's hard to be honest in front of your mate, and I understand that. Lying was probably safer for you." He ran two fingers down the side of my face, down my neck, then over my breast, letting his hand fall back to his side. "That animal would have hurt you if he knew how you really felt."

I darted my eyes around, looking for somewhere to hide. We stood in the center of a break in the shelves toward the very back of the library. Just off to the side of us, a small sitting area was positioned across from an alcove with a long table and chairs.

My heart lifted as I recognized the space. The main doors were at the end of a long stretch of shelves on the other side of the sitting area, but that meant getting past Andrus.

"Emmy!" he barked, making me jump. I snapped my eyes to him, and his tight expression softened into an ominous smile. "You've always had a hard time paying attention. Such a daydreamer. It's one of the things I love about you."

I nodded, not knowing what else to do.

He closed the space between us and ran his hands down

the sides of my arms. The material of my dress seemed to tighten, suddenly too thin in the wake of his touch.

"Andrus." I hated how weak I sounded. "I need to get back to Rin. He's probably worried."

"He doesn't care about you," Andrus said as if stating a fact. "If he truly cared about you, why isn't he here?"

I opened my mouth to argue but stopped. Where was Rin? Could he not feel my distress or fear? I was so scared I couldn't feel where he was, and my wolf spiraled. Was our mate hurt? Missing? Dead?

"I'll tell you why he isn't here. It's because he doesn't want you." Andrus licked his lips, his eyes lingering over my chest. "I understand why you'd protest against my advances, though. You're mated. Virtuous Omegas always have to resist. At least at first."

He hooked his arm around my waist and pulled me to him.

My body locked up.

Fear twisted in my chest as I realized that I had no idea what to do, where to go, or what to say.

Where the hell was my mate?

"Let me go," I whispered, my whole body trembling uncontrollably.

"Oh, Emmy," he smiled, gripping my chin and forcing me to look directly into his eyes. "I'm so sorry you were forced to mate that animal. I tried so hard to save you." He wiped at my wet cheeks. I struggled not to jerk away. "I paid that band of rogues a lot of money to save you. I'm just sorry they failed. Please forgive me."

"The rogues?" My mind was a rush of memories, and my mouth flooded with a bitter panic that made my stomach ache. "In the forest? You paid those wolves to kidnap me?"

"To save you," he continued to smile, pulling me even tighter to his blood-smeared chest. The thick red substance soaked into my blue dress, turning the fabric black. "It was my fault, really. I didn't have much time to find someone better qualified to do the job. You were taken from me so abruptly. I'm just sorry they couldn't get to you in time. I hate that that monster put his hands on you. I hope he didn't hurt you too much."

I pushed at his chest, trying to twist away, and regretted it instantly. His hard eyes bore into mine, and he jerked me hard to his firm body, pinning my arms to my sides and squeezing my ribs tight.

"Why?" I rasped, struggling to breathe properly. "Those rogues hurt my friends." I sucked in a tight breath of air, my lungs flooding with the scent of burning pine. "They killed good wolves."

"I had to, Emmy." His voice got louder, and his eyes flashed red as sheets of rain whipped hard at the windows. "I had no choice. He took you from me because of your fucking sister. That bitch ran off and sacrificed your innocence."

My wolf snarled at his horrible words, and I tried to pull my arms free, wanting to claw at his eyes, but he held me too tight. I was trapped.

"I'm here now." He swiped his nose up my cheek. "And I'm going to take you away from here, my love."

I cringed at Rin's endearment for me falling from his mouth. It sounded so wrong, so threatening.

"You don't love me," I whispered through fresh tears. My fear was taking control, and I couldn't think anymore. I could only smell Andrus' harsh scent and feel his arms locked tight around me as if I might vanish into thin air. "You have to leave, Andrus. Rin is—"

"I love you so much more than that fucker ever could!" he yelled, spraying spit into my face. His grip crushed me, and I choked on a broken sob, struggling to breathe. "I saw that animal force himself on you in the packhouse gardens. He cornered you and touched you in such an inexcusable way, where anyone could see. Then the bastard yelled at you. Abused you. He doesn't fucking deserve you, Emmy!" His eyes flashed red, and he spoke faster, his words bleeding together in his rage.

"I saw him at the temple grab you and scream at you to calm down. That's not love, Emmy. He doesn't love you!" Andrus gasped for breath as he kept rambling.

I pushed at his chest, trying to get him to let me go, but he jerked my body to him, making my head snap at the action.

"I wanted so badly to rush out and save you." His voice shifted into a deep whisper, and he pressed his nose against the side of my face. "I really did. But there were too many guards, and I didn't want to risk hurting you. So I waited. But I'm here now, my love. I'm here to save you."

"How, how long have you been in Hund Valley?" I whispered, terrified of the answer, but I needed to know exactly how long he had been watching me.

"Weeks." The word oozed from his mouth.

Moving his nose beneath my ear, he inhaled deeply. My throat tightened, and I swallowed convulsively, trying not to throw up. His tongue slipped out and dragged up and over Rin's mating bite.

I screamed.

I flung my arms out, hitting at anything and everything in front of me. Andrus released me, and I spun, not sure where to go, running blindly into the dark. My thighs instantly came into contact with the table in the alcove, and Andrus slammed his body into my back, forcing me into the unforgiving wood.

He flung me around and slammed me onto my back. The wood beneath me creaked from the force, and I gasped as pain shot up my spine.

"Calm down!" he demanded, pinning my arms over my head.

I couldn't move, the Omega in me forcing me still. I could defy Rin because it was safe, he would never hurt me, but my wolf knew better with this Alpha. He would kill me if I moved even an inch.

Andrus held my wrists with such strength. I could feel bruises forming as he squeezed. I tried kicking my feet out, but he locked my knees under one of his legs, caging me in place.

"You don't have to be scared of me, Emmy." He breathed hard as he pressed his chest into mine, his lips inches from my face. "I'm going to take care of you."

"I don't want you!" I screamed, shocking even myself. "Don't touch me! Rin! RIN!"

I tasted blood before I felt the sting of the slap across my cheek. My eyes watered, and I moved my head, trying to quiet the dizzy sensation that reverberated between my head and my stomach.

"Do you have any idea what I've done for you?" he seethed through gritted teeth. His hold on me was no longer possessive but filled with rage. It felt as if he might break my bones from the sheer force of his grip. "Do you realize how patient I've been? How hard it was to wait for you?"

I jerked my wrists, but they didn't budge. He was too strong. "Let me go," I sobbed. "I want Rin. Please, let me go."

"You bitch! You want your fucking mate? Let's see if he still wants you when I'm done."

He slapped me again, blood flooding my mouth. I choked, disoriented, feeling him jerk at the front of my dress. I heard the fabric rip and his disgusting hands wrapped around my breasts. I wanted to scream out, but my terror seized me. I couldn't move or cry.

I could only burn.

With fear, pain, and hatred.

The Fire

Rin

I RUSHED through the Omega Den, flinging open doors and checking under beds and closets. Omegas ran past me, fear and tears pouring off them. Checking the last bedroom at the end of the long hall, I found an Omega sitting on his bed crying, too scared to move.

I lowered myself to his level, trying not to add to his considerable distress. "I'm picking you up. We have to leave."

He nodded but didn't move. A few other Alphas yelled out the all-clear from other halls, and I reached for the frightened creature. He let out a startled yip but didn't fight me. Holding him tight to my chest, I gave the all-clear then raced outside.

The Elder Lodge just next door blazed, fire consuming the small building, the heavy storm doing nothing to quiet the flames. I ran to the Beta Den, a good distance from the burning building. Once inside, I settle the still crying Omega near a few Healers.

"The Den is all clear, Sir," Beta Alta said, giving me a quick bow. Her long, blonde braid swung forward, covered in soot and ash.

"Do we know what started it? Or how it got out of control so quickly?"

"No, Sir. The fire was already burning pretty hot when I got here. I had just closed up the shop and was headed home when I smelled the smoke."

"It couldn't have been an accident," Dell said, stepping up to our conversation. "It doesn't smell right."

"Something more than just wood?"

"Maybe," he scratched the stubble along his neck, "but with all the smoke, rain, and Alphas outside trying to contain it, it's hard to pinpoint the scent."

I clapped his shoulder. It wasn't the answer I wanted, but that couldn't be helped. "Thank you."

Turning, I scanned the room for the commander of the village guards, wanting a report on his men and any suspicious activity. I found him on the other side of the room, serving water to a few grateful Omegas.

I took two steps, then froze.

The air around me tensed and squeezed, pushing under my skin. Slowly, I changed direction, my body compelling me toward the doors. Once outside, I sniffed the air, pulling in the fresh scent of rain and the hard burn of smoke.

The sharp odors fell away, and a thick sense of dread filled my lungs, followed by deep confusion.

My feet started to move, and I didn't fight it. Something was pulling me toward the packhouse. Something...*off*.

The barrage of rain pushed at my shoulders as I shook my head, trying to pinpoint what was wrong. Then it hit me.

It was Emmy.

But her emotions were muted and confused. I couldn't tell if she was upset or angry or....

My bond with my Omega suddenly blazed hot, and my wolf lunged forward. He gripped my body and forced me away. My bones slid into place, dark hair rippling over my massive form. The heavy beast roared as the connection with my mate burned within me, letting me taste her fear.

I raced through the village, edging around houses and plowing into shrubs and trees, desperate to get to my mate.

The packhouse came into view, and I raced past the front door, around the side of the building. The washed-out scent of blood hit my nose as I approached the verandah next to the library. I flung myself inside the unlatched door, then stilled, listening and scenting the air.

Emmy was here somewhere. I couldn't hear her, and her scent was muted by smoke, blood, and rain, but she was here. I could feel it.

The vast, dark space revealed nothing at first. It was quiet and still. I pressed on, finding a guard a few feet from me, dead, a dagger sticking out of his neck.

My claws clacked on the polished marble as I moved, my mate's bond guiding me like a string. Another downed Alpha caught my eyes, and I edged past him, unsure if he was alive or not.

A faint trace of Emmy's scent pierced my lungs, but it wasn't right. Too sharp and...

My mate's distress slammed into me, and I started running, our bond pulling me to her.

Sprinting past several rows of books, I jumped over an awkwardly placed couch and dashed toward the back wall. I reached a break in the shelves, and my whole body convulsed at the sight before me.

Emmy was naked and pinned down onto a table, sobbing as that Casin-fuck ripped her undergarments down her legs.

He was completely naked as well, blood dripping from his chest and his cock in his hand.

Emmy struggled and tried twisting away from him, but he flung his hand high into the air and brought it down onto her face hard.

I lunged.

My jagged claws wrapped around Andrus' chest, and I tore him away from my mate.

Emmy screamed as I tore into the piece of shit. I kicked out my feet, shredding his back and legs. He twisted and flung himself backward, giving himself a sizable gap between us. I could see him trying to shift, but his body held firm. Lust did that to a wolf. It was almost impossible to let your beast take over with a raging hard-on driving your instincts.

I angled my shoulders forward, baring my teeth and letting out a fierce roar. Andrus moved his feet sideways, trying to skirt around the table, a noticeable limp in his step. His eyes shot past me, and he darted, moving right towards Emmy.

She was huddled on the floor, naked and shaking, her back pressed against a couch. She struggled to catch her breath between sobs, but she went quiet when her eyes met his.

Then she screamed.

I bolted straight for him and rammed my body into Andrus' back before he could reach her, forcing him onto the floor and away from my mate. I straddled his back, fisted his hair, and slammed his face into the polished marble. He grunted and paused for a moment before trying to throw me off. I didn't move an inch.

"Fuck you," he spat at me over his shoulder, blood spraying out over his chin. "Emmy is mine. She's—"

I didn't let him finish. I flung him onto his back and shoved my clawed hand into his mouth, forcing it downward.

He swung wildly as I pulled harder. His jaw bone popped, and he gripped my arm, trying to dig his lengthening claws into my skin. My blood seeped over his fingers, but I didn't stop. The skin on his face stretched, his eyes drooping as his flesh slowly tore. Red gashes flowed, and he choked on his own blood as I snapped off his jaw and flung it across the room, ensuring Emmy's name would never leave his lips again.

Blood gushed and bubbled from his mangled face, and he kicked out with weak legs. As much as I enjoyed seeing the pain in his eyes, I was done playing with the fucker.

I shoved my claws into his breast bone, loving the feel of it cracking and tearing open in my hands. His eyes went so wide with fear and pain. I thought they might burst.

His chest gaped open, and blood sprayed all over my black fur and across the white marble. Jerking my arms apart, I leered at Andrus' exposed, fluttering heart. Its frantic movements slowed, and I wrapped my hand around it, tearing it from his limp body.

It twitched in my hand for a moment as I brought it up to my face. The stench of his death swirled around me, thrilling my wolf, and I let out a deafening roar. Then I opened my mouth and bit down, my wolf feasting on what was left of his pathetic life.

The Alcove

Emmy

I COULDN'T LOOK AWAY, frozen in place and forced to watch as my mate ripped Andrus' jaw off his face.

Rin flung the mangled body part across the room, and it bounced off the table's leg then ricocheted toward me. It settled just near my feet, and I slowly pulled my knees to my chest, inching away from it. My body ached from the simple movement, and I couldn't help the whimper that left my lips.

A sharp crack split the air, and my eyes snapped to my mate. His wolf reached into Andrus' chest and pulled out his pulsing heart. Rin let out a fierce roar into the darkness, and I shook from the force of it, tears pouring down my face. I had never heard anything so primal or powerful in my life, and it made me want to scream.

Sinew and flesh dripped down Rin's arms as his wolf began to eat. I swallowed hard, my throat tightening and bile flooding my mouth. Despite the gore and violence, my chest warmed at the sight of my mate devouring the monster that hurt me. He was true to his word. He kept me safe.

I loved him so much.

The man, his beast, and everything in between.

A soft glow of light briefly cut through the darkness along the top of the bookshelves. Someone had entered the library. I wanted to run and warn them to stay away, but I couldn't move. I could only pray Rin didn't hurt whoever it was. At the moment, there wasn't much of his human in my Alpha, and I was so scared he wouldn't be able to stop himself from lashing out.

I let out a relieved breath as Zev came into view. He glanced at my feral mate before turning his attention to me. He moved slowly, each step soft and careful as he settled next to me, the whole time keeping a watchful eye on Rin. Zev's hands ghosted over my naked, shaking body as if he wasn't sure what to do.

He looked at Rin again, then tugged his shirt off and draped it around my shoulders. He helped me maneuver my weak arms through the sleeves and pulled the front closed, careful to keep from touching my bruised skin.

A guttural warning vibrated through the air, and I turned to Rin. His wolf snarled at Zev, bloody teeth bared, and eyes narrowed. The black wolf angled himself toward Zev, his claws sinking into Andrus' wet remains.

Zev pushed himself away from me and held his hands up in surrender.

"Rin," he whispered, keeping his eyes down and the back of his neck exposed. "It's just me. You know me. I'm your best friend, and I would never hurt Emmy. I just wanted to cover her up. She's so cold and scared."

Rin's wolf tensed as he moved his piercing, red eyes to me. His snarl faded, and he tilted his head. I shivered at the mess that dripped down his mouth and chest, but I still wanted him to hold me. Man or wolf, I didn't care which one. I just wanted him close.

"She's so scared, Rin," Zev continued, his voice so gentle. "She wants her mate. Can you help her?"

Rin's shoulders visibly relaxed, and he trembled as his fur receded and his muscles pulsed. His wolf let him go, leaving Rin naked and panting in the bloody mess of guts and bone. Slowly, he raised his head to reveal tears streaming down his face.

He looked at Zev with so much pain. "He hurt her." His voice was so weak and small. It was hard to believe it was my Rin.

"I know, my friend," Zev said, lowering his hands but not moving from his spot.

Rin looked at me, so tired and raw. I held my arms out, pushing up the blood-soaked sleeves of Zev's shirt. Rin crawled toward me, head down and shoulders hunched. He pushed his bloody face over my exposed chest and into my neck. Holding him as tightly as I could, I looked at Zev. A weak smile tugged at his lips, then he turned away, giving us a small semblance of privacy.

I inhaled deeply, Rin's scent barely discernible over the stench of metallic blood and thick smoke.

Dark streaks of gore, blood, and body parts were smeared and scattered over the bright tile. The storm continued to light up the sky, illuminating the aftermath of the violence around me.

"What do we do?" I asked Zev.

He looked around into the shadows, his brow twisted with worry and a little bit of disgust. I knew his eyes allowed him to see so much more than I could. And what I saw was horrific. I could only imagine how much more graphic it was to him.

"There's no hiding this. The Casin guard attacked you.

His death is excusable. But I don't know how the Casin Alphas will react."

I didn't know either. My father had such an odd affection for Andrus. He treated the cold Alpha more like a son than a guard, allowing him to push through the ranks despite his inexperience and age.

Rin tightened his arms around me and nuzzled his nose deeper into my neck. "If they even try to touch you," he whispered against my skin, his voice like gravel. "I'll fucking kill them all."

The Next Morning

Rin

I LAID in bed and stared at the wall. That fucking wall. I had spent so many nights staring at it the last few weeks, willing myself not to reach for the Omega sleeping next to me. Now I stared at it, trying to keep myself grounded in reality.

I had broken away from myself last night in the library. I was fused entirely with my wolf, our thoughts and needs blurring into a violent thirst for revenge. I had never experienced savagery like that before, and I hoped I never did again.

I pulled Emmy's back to my chest, careful not to wake her. Running my hands over her slight body, I brushed my fingers over the bruises on her wrists and arms. The traces of the Casin-fuck's assault mocked me for not finding her sooner. I was so stupid for ignoring my instincts and not following her myself after dinner.

This was all my fault.

"Hey there," Emmy said with a groggy rasp over her shoulder.

She rolled into me and ran her hand over the side of my face, giving me a small smile. Her cheek was a bit puffy and red, and a dark bruise lined the edge of her jaw, almost as dark as Quin's. I closed my eyes and suppressed a growl.

Quin.

"I need to find my father," I said, kissing her temple and inhaling her sugared-honey scent.

"Did you not talk to him yesterday?" she asked, running her fingers up and down my arm.

"No."

I didn't know what else to say. I failed my family. Both Omegas in my care had been viciously attacked and on the same fucking day. What kind of Alpha lets that happen?

I rolled away from my mate and grabbed a clean pair of pants. There was no sense waiting. It was probably best to confront my father before he started drinking for the day.

A fist slammed hard into the bedroom door. Emmy jumped and burrowed under the blankets as if to shield herself from the outside world.

"Yes?" I yelled, wondering who the hell could be bothering us at this hour. The sun wasn't even fully awake yet. The black night sky was just starting to turn a soft grey, the storm still lingering.

Zev pushed open the door. Dara right behind him. Both stood fully at attention, bowed low to me, and then Emmy. It was a little formal for so early in the morning.

"Alpha Rin," Zev said, and I stiffened. "It's your father. Come quickly."

I glanced at Emmy. She sat in the center of the bed, with the blanket pulled tight around her shoulders. Her wide eyes reflected my panic.

I rushed out of the room, the sound of Zev's feet not far

behind me. Racing through the packhouse, I paused when I rounded the corner to my father's quarters.

A small huddle of staff stood just outside my father's open bedroom door. His maid sobbed hysterically, choking on tears and snot. A member of the kitchen staff held her firmly, a look of distant shock on the Beta's face.

I slowed down, taking in everyone's distress and horror. Preparing myself for what I was about to find. I froze in the doorway of my father's bedroom.

His body laid across his bed, feet dangling over the edge, his stomach ripped open and spilling out over the floor. Ruddy streaks of blood decorated the walls and sheets, and indistinguishable chunks of flesh were strewn all over the bed and rug.

Everything seemed to drip with blood. Except for a single glass of whiskey, which sat undisturbed on the nightstand as if poured moments ago. The amber liquid was still and golden. It was so calm in a room full of such violent chaos.

I shoved down the thick lump that settled in my throat, very aware of the staff behind me. Moving forward to get a better view of my father's body, I immediately wished I hadn't. His attacker hadn't been kind in the least. Claw marks cut deep gashes in his arms and legs, and a sizable chunk was missing from his throat. It made me think of Andrus. I hadn't been very kind either.

"Alpha," Zev said in a very official tone. I didn't respond. He stepped closer and leaned in, whispering so no one could hear. "Are you okay, Rin?"

"I should probably cry," I whispered, my eyes refusing to leave my father. I didn't mean to sound so cold, but I was disconnected from everything in front of me.

My eyes fell on my father's lifeless face. Other than a drop of blood on the corner of his lip, his face was undisturbed. He looked as if he was napping.

Sucking in a harsh breath through my nose, I tilted my head back. *I was so fucking tired.*

"Move the Casin Alphas to somewhere more contained until we can figure out who did this," I ordered. I sounded angry, but I wasn't. I was just numb. "I want to know which staff members were in here and if anyone saw that Casin guard, Andrus, roaming around the family quarters last night. We know he was in the library, but where else did he go?"

"Consider it done." Zev's voice edged a little firmer as he continued to speak. "The temple priests are on their way to officiate your transition to Pack Alpha. And Beta Dara is preparing your mate as we speak."

Zev's eyes were sympathetic, but his words were as professional as ever. I needed it. I felt like I was going to float away at any moment, and I clung to my friend's formal demeanor and tight posture, letting it keep me grounded.

Before leaving, I turned, giving my father one last glance. His expression was soft, weathered from time and pain, but still the Alpha I remembered as a pup—strong, commanding, and loyal. And now, here he was, hanging off his bed, soaked in booze, and his chest completely fucking empty.

In the last few years of his life, the fucker didn't have a heart to speak of, so it probably shouldn't matter in death either.

The Hallway

Emmy

I FOLLOWED Rin out of Quin's room, leaving the devastated Omega sobbing in Anja's arms. I hated that the pup was mourning his father's death with his face still black and blue from the Alpha's assault.

Rin nodded at the two guards next to Quin's door, then walked briskly down the hall. I struggled to keep up, already so tired. My body hurt, and I hadn't allowed myself to think about what had happened yet.

I needed to get through the transition ceremony first. Then I'd let myself feel it.

Once Rin rounded a corner, he grabbed my arm and pulled me into a small, empty guest room. Confused, I tensed. His face was set firm and blank of all emotion like it had been all day. I thought of Zev's words in the meadow.

It's an Alpha's job to hold his people together, not fall apart with them.

Rin slammed the door shut, then tucked me gently against his chest. My body was wound so tight it took a moment before I relaxed into his strong arms, inhaling his perfect, masculine scent. He moved his big hands over my back and through my hair, soothing me.

"My love?" he whispered.

I hummed in response as I rubbed my cheek against his chest. His was so warm.

"Thank you for being so strong for me today."

I leaned back to see if he was serious. I had cried half the night, sobbed horribly with Quin, and was now on the verge of bursting into tears yet again.

"I really don't think I'd be able to do this without you." He ran his thumb over the side of my face. "Thank you."

I pushed up onto my toes as he leaned down, pressing his lips softly to mine. So safe and loved.

A knock on the door startled me, and Rin leaned back with a groan.

We hadn't been alone all morning. Priests, stewards, and guards all demanded my mate's attention and council on every little thing. I understood the chaos, but it was still overwhelming.

I set my face, thankful for our quick moment.

"Yes?" Rin's tone was just as hard as his expression.

The door pushed open, and a guard poked his head in. "Alpha Rin, the Casin wolves are ready for you."

My mate grunted in approval, then turned his fierce eyes to me. "Emyanna, wait in our room. I'll be up shortly."

"Are you going to speak with my father?"

"Yes." He motioned to someone behind me, and a guard moved just into my peripheral. "Go to our room. I'll be up shortly."

"No," I snapped. I didn't mean to sound so angry, but I was too exhausted.

I turned to the guard. "Leave."

The Alpha immediately obeyed, and Rin let out a long, rolling rumble. I was sure to be punished later for defying him in front of someone else, but I was too upset to care right now.

"That was not a request," Rin growled, his eyes flashing red.

"I deserve to speak to my father. I'm going with you." I turned toward the door and pulled it open, ignoring the fact that I had no idea where my family was being held.

"No! You are not!" Rin roared, slamming his fist hard against the door, making it slam shut with a crack. "I don't need you getting in the way."

"Get in the way of what?" I asked, my wolf cowering at the look in my mate's eyes.

"I'm certain Hector sent that piece of shit to kill my father and attack you, maybe even kill you. This will not have a peaceful ending, and you don't need to see it," he said through gritted teeth.

"What are you scared I'll see? Are you going to tear his jaw off, rip open his chest, eat his heart?" I stood firm, squeezing my hands tight.

His rage receded a bit as he stepped toward me. "That's exactly what I don't want you to see," he whispered, much softer than I expected. His eyes looked so pained as they slowly roamed my face. It was disarming.

I was so conflicted. Everything swirling inside me hurt. My veins flooded with pain for Rin, pain for Quin, pain for the guard Andrus killed in the library and the other laying in the infirmary, and now pain for me. My mate was going to kill my father. There was nothing I could do to stop him, and I wasn't even sure I wanted to, which only made me feel worse.

Overwhelmed and scared, I sniffled as a few tears escaped and fell down my face.

"I deserve to be there," I said as firmly as was possible with my bottom lip trembling. "Whatever you do," I took a steadying breath, "I deserve to speak to him first. The bruises on my body are his fault, and I'm owed at least a few minutes."

Rin looked at the floor as if expecting it to provide an answer. After a few tense moments of silence, he finally nodded. It shocked me. I didn't expect him to relent.

He walked past me and stepped quickly into the hallway, not waiting for me to follow. I ran after him, trying to keep up. His long legs moved much quicker than I was capable.

Rin rushed down the stairs, cut down a long corridor, then straight to the back offices where I never went; everything in this part of the house was used for official pack business. We reached a short hall where Zev stood next to a door flanked by two guards. Rin nodded at him, and he immediately swung it open.

"What the fuck are you playing at?" my father roared, rushing toward my mate as if he was ready to attack. Rin let out a low growl in warning, and Hector stopped in his tracks, his furious expression not faltering in the least.

I moved to step further into the room, but Zev grabbed my arm, keeping me close to his side. He gave me a knowing, somewhat apologetic look but stood firm as a barrier between me and the other wolves in the room.

"Why the hell was I woken up at an inexcusable hour and thrown in here?" Hector snarled, motioning around him as if standing in the stockades and not a tastefully decorated study. "Your men refuse to let us leave, and no one will tell me what the hell is going on? What the fuck are you playing at?"

"What do you think is going on?" I said as loudly as I could, my fury matching every bit of the Alphas around me. I stepped around Zev but stayed just next to him. "What are *you* playing at, Father?"

Hector took a small step back, and Davon's face fell from one of anger to shock.

"What?" Hector asked, shifting his gaze between Rin and me.

"You sent Andrus to ah-attack me." My voice cracked, and I hated myself for giving away my fear. "Didn't you? You had him kill Rin's father then sent him to kill me. How could you?"

"Get out," Davon snapped at the two Casin guards standing behind him. They hesitated, looking at their Pack Alpha, but Hector didn't respond. He just stared at the floor as if all thought had been pushed from his head.

"Go now!" Davon roared.

With obvious uncertainty, they both finally left, shutting the door behind them.

Hector shook his head, turning all his attention to Rin. "Rollen is dead?"

"Are you fucking kidding me?" Rin gritted out, the muscles in his neck straining. He looked like he might shift at any moment. "Are you really going to stand here and pretend you didn't know?" He let out a harsh snort. "I didn't take you for such a coward."

"Watch it, boy," Hector snarled, his features darkening and shoulders angling forward.

Zev hooked his hand under my elbow and pulled me close. I didn't fight him.

My father's eyes flashed red as he continued, "You don't have the status to speak to me in such a way."

"I can speak to you however the fuck I want, old man. I am the Pack Alpha of Hund Valley, in case you forgot." His voice dropped as he spoke, his wolf distorting his words as he struggled to stay human. "You killed my father and attacked my mate. I'm just extending you the courtesy of knowing why I'm going to rip your throat out."

"Wait!" Davon moved next to our father. His eyes were wide, and they darted to me, settling on the bruises along my jaw. "We had nothing to do with any of this. We came only to make sure Emmy arrived here in good health. That is all."

"You sound so fucking weak," Hector spat at Davon, disgust seeping out with every word.

"Then why has Andrus been here for weeks if you didn't send him ahead to scout us out?" I asked. My hands shook, but my voice didn't.

"He asked if he could escort you to Hund Valley." Davon placed a hand over his heart as if it made his words more believable. "He was only half a day behind you and was confident he'd catch up. He said that if he couldn't have you, the least he could do was make sure you arrived safely with your new mate. He seemed sincere."

Rin let out a rip of a growl, and I fought to keep from slapping my hands over my ears. "That fucker stalked her, terrorized her, beat her, and molested her. I should gut both of you for sending him my way!"

"This is such bullshit!" Hector took a step back. "You kill your father to usurp his position, which isn't shocking given the rumors I've heard, and now you're blaming it on me to keep your pack from hunting you down. I should kill you where you stand."

Davon closed his eyes and shook his head, a heavy sigh pushing out of his nose.

"Where is Andrus? I want to speak to him," Hector demanded.

"He's dead." Rin narrowed his eyes and smiled, reveling in the shocked expression that spread across my father's face.

"This, this is a calculated form of aggression," Hector said with disbelief. "You killed your mate's lover and disposed of your father, and now you blame us." He moved directly in front of Rin, trying to glare him down, but my Alpha didn't budge. "How dare you."

Zev held out an arm and gently guided me behind him. I

peeked out around his elbow, not brave enough to refuse his protection but also desperately wanting to see what was happening.

Hector pushed his head back and made his voice irritatingly loud, acting as if it gave him more authority. "I suggest you escort us out of here with a formal apology and gratitude for giving you your mate. Otherwise, I'll be forced to do something you won't like."

Rin's smirk widened.

"Don't push me, boy. This will not end well for you."

"Be careful there, old man," Rin snarled through his grin. "No one gets to speak to me like that and live to tell about it. Especially in my own house."

"I feel bad for you, Rin. I really do." Hector flashed a cocky grin. "My guard is ten times stronger than yours. Our warriors have been fighting and winning wars for centuries. And here you are mere moments from taking the reins, and your entire pack will be slaughtered. There will be nothing left for you to lead."

"Leave or die," I said, edging around Zev. He tensed but let me go. "Those are your options, Father. Either you are bound to Hund Valley and condemn Andrus for what he did to Alpha Rollen and me. Or confess what your plan was, and we'll prepare your grave. Either way, I'm done with this, done with you."

"You don't talk to me like that, you little bitch!" Hector roared.

Everything instantly fell into chaos.

Zev reached out and tugged me back. Rin rushed forward, shielding me from my father's threatening glare. And Davon yelled something at our father, but I couldn't hear over my mate's deep, horrible growls.

"One more step and I will fucking kill you!" Rin's deep voice ripped through the room, and silence settled around us.

"I have held back out of respect for my mate, but I will gut you if you so much as breathe in her direction again."

I glanced around Zev to see my father glaring past Rin, right at me. His eyes were bright red, fangs protruding from his mouth, and claws at the ready. But for the first time in my life, I wasn't scared of him. Between Rin, Zev, and even Davon, this wolf had no power to hurt me. He was the weakest wolf in the room, and his display was all for show.

Hector sucked in a deep breath through his nose, narrowing his eyes at me. "I gave you a roof over your head, food in your belly, and a mate to keep you safe. And you dare to speak to me like this? You are stupid and weak, and Casin will have its pound of flesh for your insults. I will not—" He suddenly stopped, his words seeming to stick in his throat.

Hector's face melted into a pained expression, his body going stiff and his face red. He brought a hand up and gently brushed his fingertips over his chest, back and forth.

"What?" I asked, the hairs on the back of my neck prickling.

He opened his mouth several times to speak, but nothing came out. Suddenly, he stumbled. He fell forward onto the floor and smacked his face onto the unforgiving wood. Davon stood directly behind him, a look of satisfied annoyance on his face. He glanced at me before reaching down and pulling a long blade out of my father's back. Red, foamy blood bubbled out of the wound.

My father moved his hands over the floor beneath him in a feeble manner before stilling. His sharp, slow breaths were the only sign he was still alive.

"Luna Emmy, Alpha Rin," Davon said calmly. "Please accept my apologies for the actions of my father and his guard, Andrus. I wasn't aware of my father's plan to hurt your pack in such a cowardly manner, and I hope we can move past this. I want to continue with our alliance, and I hope you do as well." He wiped the blood off his dagger and sheathed it.

Rin turned to me, his expression blank and his anger gone, at least for now. I looked down at my father dying at my feet. His blood pooled toward me, and I took a careful step back.

I was done.

With my brother, my father, and their games.

I turned to Rin and gave him a nod before walking out of the room.

The Library

Emmy

ZEV'S heavy feet followed me as I made my way back through the packhouse and toward the library. I felt compelled to see it. I needed to know Andrus' body was no longer rotting in my home and that my favorite place in the world was clean again.

The library's entryway looked the same—long rows of books and comfortable chairs, colorful art, and the sun shining brightly through the glass ceiling. It felt eerily normal.

Moving slowly toward the back, I stopped near the alcove, crossing my arms. The furniture had been pushed against the wall, and the floor was streaked with a gritty, white powder from being hastily cleaned. Only a faint trace of dried blood still settled between the marble slabs.

Zev cleared his throat before speaking. "I'm so sorry you have such horrible memories tied to this space. I know how much you loved to read here."

"I still do," I said quietly, staring at the floor. And it was true. I did still love this place, despite the horrible thing that happened here.

"I used to hide in books to escape my life. They were my comfort." I let out a breathy sigh and looked up at the heavy shelves that reached the ceiling. "The smell of books always instantly calmed my wolf. But now, this is where my mate lost his mind and ripped apart an alpha I've known most of my life." My eyes moved over the floor again. "Is it weird that I find his blood caked between the tiles comforting?"

Zev didn't say anything, his kind eyes just watching me and letting me talk.

"You killed Rin's father," I finally said, watching his reaction carefully.

He tensed, and his eyes pulsed purple for a quick moment. "No, My Lady." I wanted to believe him, but his posture was too tight. "May I ask, what makes you think that?"

"It was your shirt," I said. His pulse ticked in his neck. "Last night, you gave me your shirt. It was already soaked in blood when you got here. Before Rin touched me, I pushed up the sleeves, and they were covered in blood. You killed him."

"I didn't kill him, Luna. I give you my word."

I drew my brows together and turned to face him properly. I honestly didn't think he'd tell me the truth, but even though his words seemed honest, there was something off about the tall Alpha. There was something he wasn't saying.

"Tell me," I said. "If you didn't kill Alpha Rollen, who did?"

He hesitated, glancing over his shoulder before meeting my eyes. "Davon."

I couldn't hide my shock. It wasn't that I didn't think my brother was capable. I just didn't think he was that stupid. "How do you..."

I struggled to finish my question as my mind raced.

Zev took a careful step toward me and whispered, "I returned to the Pack Alpha's room last night after leaving Quin. I wanted to make sure he was secure in his room before turning in for the night. The door was slightly open and," he swallowed hard, but kept speaking as if compelled, "the scent of blood poured out of the room. Davon rushed out as he shifted back into his human. He moved down the hall in the opposite direction." He shook his head. "He simply didn't notice me."

Zev looked so relieved to have confessed, a bit of tension falling from his shoulders. "I saw what he had done to Alpha Rollen, then set off to find Rin. I scented him through the house and found you both in the library."

"Guards weren't stationed at Rollen's door?"

"No, ma'am," he said, squaring his shoulders and speaking a little louder. "Alpha Rollen rarely had guards on his door. Not since his mate died. He said it made him feel watched." He cocked his head. "His paranoia was pretty bad at the end."

"Will you tell Rin?" I asked, suddenly worried for Davon.

I didn't like my brother, but I loved him, and he was my blood whether I liked it or not. While he was never really kind to me, he wasn't cruel either—not like my father. But the thought of him being killed for what he had done made my heart twist. I already lost Sana, and while I probably would never see Davon again, as stupid as it was, I didn't want him dead.

"I think the real question here is," Zev said, "will *you* tell Rin?"

I gave a jerk of my head, not understanding why he wouldn't tell my mate what Davon had done.

"My Lady," Zev whispered, seeing my confusion. "Some might point out that I did nothing to pursue Davon last night after he left the Pack Alpha's room. And I did nothing to save Rollen after I found him wounded."

"Was he wounded or dead?" I asked. Zev's eyes held mine for a moment, and I shook my head. "Don't answer that."

It didn't matter, anyway. Rollen couldn't hurt Quin or torture Rin anymore, and I truly felt I might have done the same as Zev. What was done was done.

"Rollen was a good wolf," Zev said, turning his attention to the floor. "He and Lacy took me in when I had no one else. He laughed a lot and played with us when we were pups. Then Lacy got sick, and he went dim. When she died, so did he."

I watched the Alpha's face as he spoke. He looked so sad. He lost a parent today too.

He took a quick breath before speaking again. "The wolf that died last night wasn't the honorable Pack Alpha Hund Valley once knew. So," he turned to face me, "will you tell Rin?"

Fear and uncertainty pulsed hard within me. I didn't want Rin to kill Davon or punish Zev, but I couldn't lie to my mate. Not about something so important.

"You did nothing wrong, Zev," I said, letting out a pained sigh. "I have to tell Rin what Davon did. But maybe not today. He has enough to worry about today."

The Last Chapter

Rin

THE CASIN GUARDS QUICKLY REMOVED Hector's body from the packhouse. Davon lorded over his corpse as if I might attack the dead piece of shit, acting as if he wasn't the one that killed the old wolf.

The Casin guards looked angry and confused, but their aggression wasn't focused on me as much as Davon. I was sure it would be a very long and sleepless journey for the Alpha, considering the loyalties his guards were struggling with. And I briefly wondered how he'd spin this to his mother and pack once he returned. But that wasn't my problem.

All that mattered to me right now was Emmy and Quin, and they were safe.

I let out a thankful sigh at the thought, but I didn't want to enjoy my relief too much because the second you do, trouble barges in and forces you to take notice.

Moving through the packhouse, I felt it was acceptable to find my mate and fuck off for the rest of the day. The transition ceremony wouldn't be until first thing in the morning, and everything else could wait.

The stewards weren't happy with the delay, but I wasn't allowing any distractions until the Casin wolves were outside Hund Valley's borders.

Stepping into my bedroom, I found Dara laying out fresh clothes on the bed.

"Alpha Rin." She bowed low. "Luna Emmy is in the bath."

"Is she okay?" I asked. It wasn't appropriate to ask a maid something so personal of the Pack Luna, but I knew Emmy might be more open with Dara.

"This is her third bath today." She gave me a weak smile, worry creasing her brow. "She seems...restless."

"Thank you." I nodded. "You can go for the day. I'll stay with the Luna."

Dara set out a pitcher of water, and some herbs provided by Beta Sami then set off.

I moved into the washroom to find Emmy resting in the large tub with her eyes closed. Steam rose off the water's surface, flower petals floating all around her. Her dark hair was wet and framed her face so delicately. She was so beautiful.

Stepping closer, I let her honey scent mixed with lavender lull my wolf.

She sighed and pushed her lips out into a slight pout.

"My Luna," I whispered, kneeling next to her.

She peeked her eyes open and smiled. "My Alpha."

"Tell me, my love," I tucked a strand of hair behind her ear, "how are you?"

"I'm okay," she whispered, but she wasn't. I could feel it.

"Do you want to lay with me in bed? No touching," I said, not wanting to aggravate her injuries. The bruises on her wrists were very dark, and a few lighter ones were still forming near her ribs.

"No touching?" she pouted.

I chuckled at her adorable puffed-out cheeks. "I know you've been through a lot, and I don't want to hurt you or make you feel worse. I just want to be near you. It's been a rough couple of days."

"That sounds lovely," she said, a sense of relief pushing off her.

I grabbed a towel and wrapped her up, carrying her to our bed. She snuggled in while I stripped down.

The truth was, I didn't need to take her in a primal way. I really did just want to hold her.

I was so wound up and raw, and I hadn't had the chance to think about my father's death, Quin now being my sole responsibility, or the trauma Emmy had endured. I was running off adrenaline and anger, but now I could lay with my mate and just let all of it settle in my head.

Emmy nestled under the blankets, pushing and patting them into place. Her nerves were so shot the urge to nest took over, and I patiently waited while she worked. Once she set everything just so, she turned to me and held out her slender arms, inviting me in. I pushed my way under the blankets, careful not to disturb the shape.

Emmy immediately pulled me to her. I laid my head on her shoulder and hummed as she ran her fingers through my hair.

"How are you?" she asked, letting out a soft breath as I nuzzled her neck.

"I'm better now. But I'm worried about you."

She pulled back slightly, her bright eyes shining down on me. "I would be lying if I said I was fine, but I think I'm still numb to it. I'm happy all those horrible Alphas are gone. So many awful wolves died *in our house*. It's weird, but it makes me feel better too." She paused, a look of distant worry on her face. "Does that make me evil?"

"No." I shook my head. "It's not evil to want to be safe."

"Rin," she whispered, fear suddenly flooding her beautiful eyes. "Uhm, Davon, he...he was the one—"

"Emmy," I cut in, knowing she needed to talk about what happened but feeling selfish in my grief. "Can we not talk about him or any of the political pack stuff right now? If you need to talk about what happened to you, I'm here, my love. But right now, Davon is on his way to Casin, and that's where I'd like to keep him. Out of my house."

Her features softened, and she let out a thankful breath. "Honestly, I don't want to talk about him either." She gifted me a small smile. "I'm sorry."

"No need to be sorry, my love." I placed a quick kiss to the mating bite on her neck, running my nose just beneath her ear. "We can talk about him tomorrow. But today is just for us."

She leaned into my movements, humming as I nuzzled her cheek. I wanted to pull all the pain and worry out of her mind and body. But I'd have to settle for just holding her. Hopefully, that would help, even just a little.

"Rin?" my mate whispered, her voice laced with a touch of unease.

"Yes?"

"Will you...touch me?" Her big eyes were so sad and scared. I couldn't have said no if I wanted to. "I hate that he was the last one to touch me like that. I need you to put your hands on me and replace those awful memories. I want you."

"Are you sure?" I was a little scared of hurting her. Beta Sami said she was more or less in good health, considering what happened, but I didn't trust that her injuries were so slight. Her bruises were too dark.

"I don't want you to push yourself," I said. "I really don't need anything other than to hold you."

"I need more, though. Please."

She leaned in and placed a soft, lingering kiss on my lips. I didn't move, letting her touch and kiss me as much as she needed. Slowly, she trailed small feather-like kisses across my face and down my neck. She ran her nose over my throat up to my ear, inhaling deeply.

I closed my eyes, leaning into the sensation of my Omega scenting me. It was so relaxing and sweet until I felt it—a small, delicate, kitten-like swipe of her tongue just beneath my ear. I was instantly hard.

Shifting slightly, I looked down at my mate. She stared up at me with half-lidded eyes filled with so much love and trust.

"Touch me," she whispered, her voice low and sexy.

I leaned back against the mound of pillows, then reached for her. "Come here."

Confusion spread across her delicate features as I guided her to straddle me. As much as I'd prefer to take her, it was more important to be careful of her injuries, and I wasn't confident I would be able to hold back from fucking her ragged.

Her small body settled, my cock flat against my stomach, her pussy hugging the shaft.

"Take what you need," I said, loving the feel of her on top of me.

Placing her hands carefully on my chest, she looked down at the crown of my cock sticking out between her thighs. Uncertainty flittered across her features as she tentatively settled her weight on me. It was unusual for Omegas to take the lead in the bedroom, and I smiled, remembering her still considerable inexperience.

"Need some help?" I asked, not wanting her to feel self-conscious.

She nodded, struggling to meet my eyes.

Sitting up, I wrapped my arms around her. Rubbing my nose gently over her throat, her scent washed over and through me, settling my wolf and thickening my cock even more.

"Hmmm," I growled. "You smell so good."

I gently licked at my mark, not wanting to rush anything should she change her mind, but I also prayed she wouldn't.

Kissing along her jaw, I moved up to her ear, gently nipping at her earlobe. She let out a breathy gasp, and I fell into her, sucking hard at my mating bite and devouring her sweet scent.

"You taste so good." I squeezed her ass and pulled her hips, gliding her wet cunt over my cock.

She pulled at my shoulders, bringing me closer to her delicate body. "Rin. Please," she moaned.

Laying back, I gripped her hips and guided her up. "Put my cock inside you."

Slowly, with uncertain movements, she reached between her thighs and grabbed the base, slipping the head between her puffy lips. We both moaned as she eased down.

Inch by inch, she sat on my thick member, holding herself deep, then she moved. Shuddering, she rocked her hips experimentally.

"Rin, I never...oh my..." Her head fell back, and sweet whimpers left her throat.

"You like that?" I asked, squeezing her breasts. Her nipples puckered at my touch, and it took everything in me not to force her onto her back and drive into her like an animal.

"Alpha," she gasped, circling her hips, instinctively letting her body satisfy her needs. "Is this okay?"

"Keep going, Omega. Fuck yourself on my cock."

Using my thumb, I circled her hard, little clit, so fucking wet, and she let out a wild moan. Confidence growing, Emmy built up her momentum. She dropped her hands onto my chest for leverage, bouncing hard and fast on my cock.

Everything about the sight before me was a fucking feast—her blown-out eyes, wild hair, and the slight jiggle of her tits with each jerk of her hips.

My knot started to expand, and her slick gushed as she came, covering my cock and groin.

Unable to help myself, I thrust up into her, fucking her right.

Emmy's eyes rolled, and she tilted her head back, letting out a passion-filled scream. Her breasts bounced to my rough movements, and her thighs shook.

Digging my fingers into her plush ass, I shoved her down onto my cock, taking her hard and fast as she came.

My knot expanded as her body went limp, falling over my chest.

I continued to fuck up into her, shoving her sweet cunt onto me and sealing us together as I came hard, spilling deep inside my delirious mate.

Gently rocking her hips over me, I prolonged her climax for as long as I could, not stopping until her pussy stopped clenching me.

Flipping us, I kissed her deeply, running my hand between her breasts. I loved the intense difference between her pounding heart, beating wildly against my palm, and her limp body, unable to move beneath me.

I caressed, kissed, and whispered soft praises, loving everything about her. Her sweet skin, her gentle heart, and her passionate temper. She was so fucking perfect.

Once my knot deflated, I moved to roll off her.

"No," she whispered, her voice breathy and light, draping her arms around my neck.

"I don't want to crush you."

She tightened her hold and pulled me down onto her

body. "I like you on top of me," she pouted. "Stay and love me. Don't go."

"I won't go." I kissed the corner of her lips and ran my fingers through her soft hair. "I'm right here, my love. I'll always be here. I promise."

NEED MORE **EMMY** AND **RIN**? Sign up for my newsletter at kittlynn.com to get access to a sweet and sexy *epilogue* of these two.

Need More?

INTERESTED IN **QUIN** and **Zev's** love story? Read their book, Fated.

WANT to find out what happened to **Sana**? Read her book, Sana's Escape.

WANT to find out what happens when easy-going **Dell** meets **Elora**, a feisty, wild Omega? Read their story, Feral.

THANK YOU FOR READING!

It means so much to me that you read my little book. I hope you enjoyed this story as much as I enjoyed writing it. If you did, it would be so lovely if you could write a short review on your favorite book website. Reviews are so important for authors and even just a single line can make a big difference. Thank you so much!

Also by Kitt Lynn

The Broken Omega Series

The Last Rose

Violet Flames

Threats of Jasmine

Marigold Run

Consider the Lilies

The Hund Valley Series

An Alpha's Promise

Fated

Feral

Tethered

The Blushing Moon Trilogy

Until The Moon Ends

The Blue Path

Broken Stars

The Casin Village Series

Sana's Escape

Davon's Salvation

Demi's Guardian

The Madra Series

A Winter Gift

Spring Blossoms

Ruined Summer

Novellas

About the Author

Kitt lives in Oklahoma with her husband and stacks on stacks on stacks of fantasy books.

She is obsessed with fantasy, fairylands, love stories, and horror in general. If you dig these things then you might enjoy her books. You can find pictures of her sweet puppies, her coffee obsession, and the ridiculous things she says to keep herself motivated on her Instagram @kittlynnauthor.

Join my free newsletter to enter giveaways and receive exclusive content! Please visit
kittlynn.com

g goodreads.com/kittlynnauthor

⊙ instagram.com/kittlynnauthor

♪ tiktok.com/@kittlynnauthor

BB bookbub.com/profile/kitt-lynn

www.ingramcontent.com/pod-product-compliance
Lightning Source LLC
Chambersburg PA
CBHW051627260626
47170CB00004B/1075